COWBOY JACKPOT: VALENTINE'S DAY

BY RANDI ALEXANDER

to Suzanne,
Enjoy the ride!
Randi Alexander

Cowboy Jackpot: Valentine's Day

By Randi Alexander

Edited by E.L Felder

Chapter One

Dallas Burns shifted on the plush chair in the high-stakes area of the Old West Casino in Las Vegas. He tipped his black cowboy hat back on his head and glanced around the red velvet-lined room.

Hell, he hoped his buddies didn't see him playing roulette. Not that it was a woman's game or anything, but rodeo men only talked about poker. The way they liked to tease each other, this would be a tough one to live down.

"Twenty-four black." The dealer set five more chips on Dallas's bet on Black, and five on his Even bet.

He scooped up his winnings and stacked them in front of him. He'd been fascinated with the game since he was a kid watching an old cowboy movie. Tonight, he was having the best luck of his life. He did a quick count. He had over six thousand dollars in chips and he'd started with three hundred.

He set five chips on First Twelve, and five on Odd. Mixing it up had been working for him tonight. The table was busy. Seven other people stood or sat around the board and placed bets that were quite a bit larger than his. A few wrists flashed diamond-studded watches as they set down their chips.

He glanced around the room and caught a very familiar green gaze.

Kira Morrow. Her eyes opened wide and she leaned toward the strawberry blonde next to her, pointed at him, and said something he knew couldn't be good.

Kira wore a soft-looking blue sleeveless dress and low-heeled white sandals that matched the little purse hanging on her shoulder. It was nearly noon, had they been out on the strip? Her bright red hair hung loose and shimmery halfway down her back. He'd loved running his fingers through it two months ago at Christmas. The day his buddy Boone had met his fiancée, Gigi, right here in this same casino.

Dallas, Boone, and his brother Jayden, had been competing in a rodeo put on for local charities. They'd driven down from Reno for a few days, and had run into Gigi and Kira, who they'd mistaken for buckle bunnies.

Dallas looked back at the table, hoping she would keep walking. He and Kira had gotten into a nasty dust-up on Christmas Day. She'd stormed off and flown back to New York before he'd had a chance to cool down and apologize.

Her unmistakable floral scent threaded through his nostrils and into his brain, making his body remember how he'd wanted her crazily back then. He turned his head. "Kira."

"Dallas." She stood right next to him, too close for safety.

She looked better than ever, her long body slim and graceful, her beautiful breasts large and round.

"Stop staring at my tits."

A couple people at the table laughed.

He met her gaze. "Then get them the heck out of my face."

She lifted a brow. "As charming as ever, I see." She gestured to his other side. "This is my cousin Stormie."

He turned and started to rise.

"Oh, don't get up." Stormie pressed her hand on his shoulder, keeping him down. She was strong. Her denim shorts showed toned legs ending in flip flops, and her white tank top displayed some noticeable but feminine arm muscles.

He held out his hand to her. "My condolences for being attached by blood to this…sweet lady."

Stormie giggled and shook his hand, then leaned closer to Dallas. "She's always been mean, but now I'm big enough to fight back."

He took a closer look at her. Green eyes like Kira's, pale skin with cute freckles. Much too young for him, but he liked her spunk. "Are you here for the bachelorette party?"

"Dallas?" Kira interrupted. "Can I play a chip?"

He turned his head. "Sure." He could afford to lose one chip to get Kira less irritated with him. He needed to work on accomplishing that before they had to walk down the aisle together in New York next week, at Boone and Gigi's wedding.

"I am going to the bachelorette thing." Stormie drew his attention. "I hadn't planned on it so Kira and I were just out shopping. I'm here with my parents for the stock show. When I heard Kira would be here too, we arranged to meet. We had drinks with Gigi last night and she invited me to the party tonight."

Dallas nodded. She worked with stock, probably rode a horse. That's where her well-shaped curves came from.

"What kind of stock do you raise?"

"Horses, mostly, and we've diversified into bucking broncs."

"I've met a few of those." He cracked his neck, relieving the tightness from an old injury.

"Oh right, now it clicks. You're a bronc rider." Stormie grimaced. "When Kira saw you, and told me your name, I didn't place you right away."

More than likely because Kira had been saying something insulting about him.

The dealer spun the wheel and set the ball rolling. "No more bets," he called. "No more bets."

Dallas glanced at the table. All his chips were gone. "What the fuck?"

The chips stood in a tall stack on one spot on the roulette table.

"Kira." His heart palpitated and sweat broke out on his forehead. "Why?"

She smirked. "I put them all on double zero, 'cause you're a big old crusty double zero in my opinion."

Curses rained through his head, followed by a vision of grabbing her long, pale neck and choking the life out of her. Then he felt the need for tears. "Damn it to hell, woman." He grabbed her wrist. "Do you know how much that was?"

She rolled her eyes and tugged her arm free. "You big baby. What was it? Fifty bucks? I'll pay you back." She huffed out a breath and opened her purse.

"More like six thousand."

She froze and her eyes widened. "Say that again." Her cheeks flushed a peach color as she tipped her head.

"Double zero." The dealer's voice called. "Double zero's the winner."

Dallas was so focused on Kira and his lost money, it didn't register right away.

"You won!" Stormie jumped up and down. "Dallas, you won!" She squealed like a little girl.

Cheers and applause boomed around the table.

Dallas sat staring. "I won?"

The pit boss came over with a small computer and typed. The dealer counted Dallas's chips, then the two men stared at the computer.

The pit boss looked at Kira. "Congratulations. You've won one hundred ninety six thousand dollars."

Dallas opened his mouth but nothing came out.

Kira pointed to him. "They're his chips."

"My chips," he repeated, his brain still dazed.

"Sir." He looked at Dallas. "Did you authorize her to bet your chips?"

"I did, but I didn't think she'd—"

The pit boss nodded. "She placed the chips. The jackpot is hers."

Dallas stood so fast his chair fell backward. "What?" His voice echoed through the room. He turned to Kira.

She gave him a malicious smile, looked back at the pit boss, and asked, "Can I get that wired right into my checking account?"

Dallas shook his head. The woman was

beautiful, sexy, frustrating, and asking for trouble. "Kira."

****

Kira let the smile fall from her face. The disappointment in his voice ruined all her fun.

Stormie grabbed her arm. "You're not going to take his money, are you?"

Kira looked into Dallas's black eyes. "I don't know." She didn't need the money. Stormie knew her parents were wealthy, but no one knew that Kira had inherited when she'd turned twenty-three. Inherited a lot. She just wanted to keep him close for a while. Get to know who he really was behind that rough surface. "I'm willing to discuss it with you." She lifted her brows and gave him a grin.

Dallas visibly unclenched his jaw as someone picked up his overturned chair. "What do you mean discuss it?" His hands fisted.

She hoped to spend time with him, not make him so angry he'd...hit her? She shook her head.

Last Christmas, when Kira had her family attorney's private investigator do background checks on him, Boone, and Boone's brother Jayden, she'd found out Dallas had been accused of assault. Just last month, the investigator let her know that he'd been found not guilty. Did that really mean he was innocent, though?

"Kira?" He leaned closer. "Tell me what you're planning."

The look he gave her sent up warning signals in her brain, but she wanted to give him a chance. At Christmas, he was as amazing a person as she'd ever met. Serious and intelligent, quietly sensual. At least, that's how he'd been before things got ugly between them.

"The casino says the money is mine. You think it should be yours, right?"

His eyes narrowed and he nodded. "Rightfully."

"Legally, it's mine, which trumps your 'rightfully,' doesn't it?" She shook her head. She shouldn't tease him any longer. "But I agree with you. You have a right to it."

He just stared, but he unfisted his hands.

"Hi, I'm Michelle, your casino host." A petite woman in a dark suit stepped up to them. "Congratulations on your win."

A cork popped. "Champagne, compliments of the Old West Casino." Glasses were filled and handed to the three of them as well as to the other players.

"Free champagne." Stormie grinned. "This is so cool."

Dallas glanced at her then back at Kira. "Is she old enough to drink?"

"I'm twenty-two." She tapped her glass to Kira's, then to Dallas's. "Congratulations to whichever one of you wins this battle."

The casino host gestured to someone behind her. "We'd like to take a few photos, then we'll get you settled in the manager's office to fill out your paperwork."

A photographer stepped closer, the casino host arranged them in front of the roulette table, and said, "Smile."

Turning toward the camera, Dallas's lips curved slightly upward. Evidently his version of happiness.

Kira grinned and turned on every watt of charm she had. Leaning into Dallas, the firm, hot muscles of his arm burned into her through his fancy western-cut shirt. The dark blue pattern hit her as extra macho as it lay against his tan skin, and the tuft of dark hair showing at his chest made her gooey inside. The photographer snapped away as Kira remembered those biceps from Christmas. He had moved in for a kiss and she'd grabbed him to push herself away.

Half blinded by the flashes, her memories of his sexy face drawing closer to her sent warm rushes of desire into her belly. She rubbed a little closer to him and her hand brushed where his dark jeans covered his sexy ass.

He put his hand on her lower back. "Don't even think you can seduce me out of all that money, woman."

Sucking in a breath, she let her body tingle with the excitement of his touch. She turned to him. "You'd better play by my rules, Dallas, or you're not going to see a penny of it."

His head swiveled to face her. "A man has his pride, Kira. You push me too far…"

"And?" Was he threatening her?

"And I'll tell Gigi what you're up to." He tried to fight back a smile.

Relief flowed through her. "That's not even fair," she teased.

"I have a suite for you two." The casino host's smile looked a little unsure.

Kira wiggled closer to Dallas. "Are you telling us to get a room?"

The woman blushed and winked. "I sure am." She gestured. "Come with me and we'll get you all set up."

Kira turned to Stormie, who was having her champagne flute refilled by a handsome casino employee. "Meet me in the Roundup Bar? And would you call Gigi and see if she can be pried away from her fiancé long enough to have a drink with us?"

Stormie nodded. "I'll see you there. Wait…" She pulled Kira aside and her face turned serious. "Dallas seems like a nice guy, under all the teasing. You're not going to screw him out of his money, are you?"

Her cousin, the church-going, all-American, Oklahoma cowgirl. Always everyone's conscience. One of the things Kira loved about her. "No. I'm just making him sweat a little. Call it…payback."

With a smile, Stormie waved her off. "Don't push too hard, or you may find him gone."

Kira took the words to heart as they left the table followed by another chorus of congratulations.

Dallas kept his hand on her lower back and the contact spread warmth through her. She liked him, and had thought of him much too often as she'd finished her master's degree in New York, and prepared to move into a position at her family's accounting firm. A job she'd accepted only because she didn't know what she really wanted to do with her life.

"You are lucky." The casino host used her keycard to unlock a discreet door that led to a bright hallway. "I've never seen that large a win on roulette." A security guard sat on a tall stool inside the door.

"Stupid luck." Dallas ushered Kira in ahead of him.

Her heels clicked on the tile floor, echoing on the walls and ceiling.

Smiling at them, the woman asked, "Why stupid?"

He looked at Kira. "What should have been the end, wound up being just the beginning."

Kira drifted deep into the intensity of his dark eyes. His words swirled like sweet chocolate through her brain. Just the beginning.

He took her arm. "Kira, wait."

She stopped and glanced up at him.

Dallas half-smiled at the casino host. "Could we have just a few minutes?"

The woman looked at her for confirmation. When Kira nodded, the host gestured down the hallway. "I'll just be at the end and to the left. Take your time."

Watching her go, Dallas drew Kira further from the guard before releasing her arm. "Let's settle this right now." The space between his eyebrows wrinkled. "Are you going to take the jackpot?"

An ache formed behind her heart. "Do you really think I'm that much of a bitch?"

He shook his head and his eyes softened. "No, you're not a bitch. But I know you're riled at me, and have been since Christmas." He huffed out a breath. "I looked for you after we had that disagreement in the lobby bar, but you were already gone."

"Why were you looking for me?" The ache turned to hope.

He looked down and scuffed one cowboy boot

on the floor. "I owe you an apology." His head came up. "I overreacted, and I'm sorry."

A burst of delight surprised her. "I owe you an apology right back, cowboy." She moved closer. "Not for doing a background check, because that was something I did for Gigi. What I'm sorry for is accusing you of looking like you wanted to…hit me." The words she'd flung at him still burned her throat.

His lips curved into a frown. "I was angry. I'll admit that was a rough time in my life, but that's no excuse for me to frighten anyone. You." He took her hand. "I didn't mean for you to feel threatened, and I apologize for that, too."

She wanted to tell him she knew he'd been found not guilty, but it would sound like she'd been keeping track of him, and that would fire off another round of pissed-off.

Tipping her head, she sighed. "We didn't do too well at Christmas. Maybe Valentine's Day will be luckier for us?"

He lifted her hand and kissed her knuckles. His eyes, shadowed under his hat, carried heat that sizzled through her bloodstream. "It's started out pretty damn lucky, don't you think?"

She nodded. "And speaking of luck, how about splitting the jackpot?"

He smiled, the first real one she'd seen from him today. "Exactly what I was thinking. I provided the stake, you provided the luck. Fifty-fifty?"

She nodded. Was it luck, though? By moving all his chips to double zero, she'd been trying to taunt him into revealing his true nature. He'd been angry, but he hadn't reacted physically, besides lightly gripping her wrist.

If it wasn't luck, was it fate giving her another chance at Dallas?

"Fifty-fifty." She said as his phone rang.

He slid it from his pocket. "It's Jayden. Okay if I take it?"

"Of course. I'll go find—"

Still holding her hand, he tugged her back to him and wrapped an arm around her shoulders and started walking with her as he answered the phone. "Hey." He grinned. "Yep, you heard right." He raised an eyebrow at whatever Jayden said. "We're doing the paperwork now. We just went through a hidden door near the gift shop and are heading to meet with the money guy." He listened for a minute. "Yep, or meet us in the Roundup in fifteen minutes or so." He disconnected.

"Thanks for doing this, Kira."

"For sharing what is rightfully yours?"

"Rightfully, not legally. Big difference."

She laughed. Maybe he was the man she'd hoped he was.

The meeting with the manager went quickly. He agreed that they could split the jackpot, and he had them fill out some paperwork. He explained that the Gaming Commission needed to verify the jackpot before the money could be released. That would probably take until morning. He gave Kira and Dallas his business card and asked them to call him any time after nine a.m. He'd meet them in the casino and bring them to his office to finalize the payments.

Kira and Dallas walked back along the bright hallway carrying keycards to the Wrangler Suite. The cards were loaded with a total of five hundred dollars in casino credit for the bars, restaurants, and room service.

Kira wanted to get him alone for a while, locked in the suite together so they could get reacquainted, rewind to that point when they were wild about each other, and hungry for more.

An idea formed, a way to show him who she really was, how sincere she was in her apology, and how interested she was in…a future? She stopped and looked at him. How was she imagining a future with a bronc rider from Reno, when her life was mapped out for her in New York?

"What's wrong?" Dallas stopped next to her.

"I forgot something. My…pen." She smiled at the security guard. "In the office. It'll just take a second." She walked backward a few steps.

The guard nodded.

She looked at Dallas. "I'll be right back." She turned and quick-stepped back the way they'd come. A future? Oh God, what was she doing?

Chapter Two

Dallas watched Kira trot down the hallway, her heels clomping, her hair flying. "What the fuck?"

She hadn't used her own pen. The manager had given them each a souvenir casino pen, his with a cowgirl who stripped, hers with a cowboy who did the same.

He'd wait for her, let her do whatever she was up to… "Aw fuck." Was she changing her mind? Telling the casino guy she wanted all the money, didn't want to split it with him? He shook his head. She wouldn't do that.

He shoved his hands in his back pockets and paced. She wouldn't, would she? After their apologies, after wanting a fresh start. "Hell." He fought the urge to go after her, listen to what she was telling the guy, but that wasn't the right thing to do. He pushed open the door into the casino and stepped out, waiting for it to lock him out so he couldn't change his mind and go confront her. Damn, that woman made him pure loco.

He spotted Jayden leaning against a slot machine chatting up a brunette cocktail waitress. She leaned into him and touched the sleeve of his red Western-cut shirt.

Jayden had to look up at her from under his cowboy hat. In three-inch heels and fishnet stockings, her legs went on forever. Her costume, fashioned after that of the saloon girls of the old West, was more like a swimsuit with fringe sewn on.

Jayden gestured to Dallas, took a slip of paper from the waitress, and sauntered over to him. "Hey, rich man. How'd it go?"

Dallas took a breath. "She's up to something."

His friend's dark blue gaze slid the door Dallas had come out of. "Where is she?"

He jerked his head. "Said she forgot something and went back in." Doubt clouded his thoughts. "You think she could be plannin' a double-cross?"

Jayden's eyes narrowed. "She doesn't seem like the type, but then, money can make people do strange things." His brows lifted. "'Course, you know that."

His gut clenched at the memory of his last girlfriend, her promises, her lies, her perjury. "I sure as fuck do."

"What are you gonna do?" Jayden pulled off his cowboy hat and ran his fingers through his curly blond hair.

What could he do? She held all the power. She'd offered to give him half the money, even told the casino manager that she'd just take half. But now that she'd run back to the man's office… "Hell, I'm gonna have to stick on her like a burr."

Jayden's mouth quirked. "Sounds like fun."

It did sound like fun. Naughty, sexy, long hours keeping an eye on her while holding her close to him, under him, in a big, soft bed. He pulled out the keycard. "Kira and I got a suite, so you've got the room to yourself tonight."

"Aw gee, what'll I do all by myself?" He held up the slip of paper the waitress had given him. "Krissie gets off at six tonight."

"Watch out, Jay. Tomorrow's Valentine's Day." He slid the card into his pocket. "You don't want to get tangled up in all that mushy shit."

Jayden frowned. "I like all that mushy shit." He pocketed the number. "You're the one who needs to get mushy if you intend to stick to Kira until tomorrow."

He hadn't thought of that. What if she wanted to skip the suite, skip him?

"I guess I'll have to use some cowboy charm to keep her around." It wouldn't be a hardship. He'd wanted her the moment he'd seen her on Christmas Eve.

Jayden snorted. "Cowboy charm? You?" He shook his head. "You ain't got none of that."

"Fuck if I don't." True, he wasn't as cute as Jayden, or as funny as Boone, but he had his own way with the ladies. Dark and brooding one of them had called him.

"Yeah, if staring them down and freezing them with that bear growl of yours is considered charming."

"Bear growl?" His voice rolled low and hard. Like a bear. "I've got plenty of moves." He glanced at the door, but it remained shut.

Jayden's eyes showed surprise. "Yeah?" He resettled his hat on his head and stuck his thumbs into his front pockets.

"Yeah," Dallas growled. Aw hell, he could use all the help he could get with Kira. Most of the women he'd been with over the last ten years were buckle bunnies or one-nighters from bars. What did he know about seducing a classy lady from New York?

Jayden couldn't keep girls from crawling all over him. What did he know that Dallas didn't?

"All right, Romeo. Show me your best move." He held up a hand. "But if you tell anyone I asked, you won't be ridin' any rodeos for a while."

"Righteous strategy, Dallas. Ask for my help then threaten me."

"Forget it." He turned. "Just fucking forget it." He felt like an idiot asking a twenty-year-old for dating advice.

Jayden laughed. "Naw, c'mon. This'll be fun." He winked. "And our secret."

Dallas rolled his eyes. "Great." This was not going to be any variety of fun.

"Listen. For starters, smile." He curled his lips up and showed his teeth. "This is what it looks like."

Dallas crossed his arms over his chest. "You're such a little shit, Jayden."

"I'm serious. Smile. Chicks love it."

Kira had teased him back in December about his sober face that never loosened up. He looked at his buddy and forced a grin.

Jayden flinched. "Oh man. You'll need to practice that in a mirror."

Pursing his lips, he gave his friend a glare. "What else?"

"Body language." Jayden looked down at where his thumbs rested in his pockets and his hands bracketed his package. "Where does this draw a woman's eye?"

Dallas snorted a laugh. "Really?" He uncrossed his arms and mirrored Jayden's pose.

"Good." Jayden shifted and leaned against the side of a slot. "A little hip."

"What are you, a stripper?"

"Hip. Loose. Not tight-assed."

Dallas gave it a try. "I think I dislocated something."

"Buddy, makin' you into a chick magnet is gonna take a whole lot more time than we have right now."

The door to the back of the casino opened and Kira walked out. Jayden dropped his hands and moved away a step.

Kira's gaze shot to Dallas, jerked down to his fly, then back up to meet his eyes with a sexy smile.

"Told ya," Jayden whispered.

"Damn," he breathed as he returned Kira's smile with a real one, a result of the excited beat of his heart and the hum of desire rolling low in his gut.

She strode up to them holding a gold pen in her hand. "Got it." She reached for Jayden. "Hi, Jay. How are you?"

"A heck of a lot better now that you're here." He leaned in for a half hug.

Kira squeezed him with a sigh. "I've missed you."

Dallas's jaw clenched. The kid had better watch his hands.

"Congrats." Jayden backed away. "Looks like you two will be sharing a nice chunk of change."

Her eyes dropped for a second before she nodded. "Yes. Hard to believe, isn't it?"

Worry tightened in Dallas's stomach. She was up to something.

Jayden had caught her nervousness, too. After a meaningful glance at Dallas, he hitched a thumb over his shoulder. "Boone and Gigi said they'd meet us at the Roundup."

"Let's go." Kira started walking and the cowboys flanked her. "I could use a drink."

"Yep. Me, too." Both Kira and Jayden looked at him. He practiced a smile and Kira returned it. He took her hand and she sighed. Yep, sticking close to her was going to be a pleasure.

They walked into the Roundup Bar and Stormie waved and slid down off her barstool.

Jayden let out a slow whistle and used one finger to tip his hat back.

Stormie walked toward them, her long, firm legs looking smooth as her round hips swayed a fascinating rhythm. Dallas hadn't noticed her nicely shaped breasts before, but evidently, Jayden saw them now.

"Buckle bunny dead ahead," Jayden murmured.

Kira stiffened.

"Jay, hold on." Dallas held tighter to her hand in case she let loose on Jayden with an uppercut. "That's Kira's cousin."

"Really." He drawled the word slowly.

Stormie's freckled face glowed and her smile showed perfect teeth. Her long, strawberry blonde hair floated behind her. "Jayden Hancock." She stopped in front of him and held out her hand. "I'm so excited to meet you."

Jayden moved a little closer as he took her

hand. "You can bet I'm just as excited to meet you." His grin could have turned a nun naughty.

"Wow." Stormie breathed the word as her green eyes took in Jayden's face.

Kira elbowed Dallas. "Wow is right. What are we witnessing here?"

Whatever it was, it looked like something they shouldn't be watching. "Let's get a table." Dallas put his hand on Kira's back and guided her to the big round booth they'd shared with Boone, Gigi, and Jayden at Christmas.

Kira slid in while keeping an eye on Jayden and Stormie, who seemed to be deep in conversation.

Dallas sat next to Kira. "Don't worry about Jay. He looks dodgy, but he's virtually harmless."

"I'm not worried about him. I'm worried about Stormie." She wrinkled her brow. "I've never seen her like that around a guy before."

Dallas didn't see anything wrong with Stormie's behavior. At the roulette table, she'd been energetic and charming. The same as she was now with Jayden. "She's a rodeo fan?"

"Uh huh." Kira tapped her finger on the table. "I'd mentioned all your names last night, but she didn't seem to be a fanatic. Just a fan."

Stormie and Jayden stood close together, talking like they were old friends.

Dallas watched them for a minute. "She hasn't tackled him and ripped off his clothes yet, so I think they'll be okay without direct supervision."

Kira relaxed back onto the padded seat. "You're right. They're adults."

He lifted a brow. Dallas sure didn't see Jayden

as an adult, yet. The kid was only twenty, but he had a fake ID. Hell, Dallas was eight years older, and he barely felt like an adult, himself.

Boone and Gigi walked into the bar. Boone resembled his little brother, Jayden, but with straight, shaggy blond hair and lighter blue eyes. His wiry bull rider's body was decked out in cowboy boots, jeans with a big championship belt buckle, and a black T-shirt.

Gigi, shorter and very curvy, wore a red sundress and white sandals. Her long, black hair looked mussed, as if Boone had kissed her very recently. Like in the elevator on the way down to the casino.

Dallas envied his friend's perfect life with the woman who made him so damn happy.

Jayden introduced Stormie to Boone. Gigi already knew her. They all wandered over to the booth.

"Congratulations." Boone shook Dallas's hand as Gigi slid in next to Kira. "What've you got planned for the money?" Boone eased into the back of the booth next to Gigi.

Stormie piled in by Boone, and Jayden took the end seat next to her, sitting a little closer than the spacious booth required.

Dallas grinned. "I'm thinkin' about investing it in a rodeo school somewhere north of here."

For years, Dallas, Boone, and Jayden had been planning to convert the Reno farm Boone inherited, into a rodeo school for bull and bronc riders.

Boone nodded. "I know just the place." He'd already invested his half of the jackpot he'd split with Gigi into updating the barn into a regulation size arena.

Gigi leaned her shoulder into Boone's. "We'll all be partners." Gigi had thrown in her winnings, too, and was currently a half-partner in the venture. "How much was your win? Stormie said almost two hundred thousand?"

Dallas slung his arm across the back of the booth and touched Kira's shoulder. "Half of that." He narrowed his gaze on her, watching for signs of dishonesty. "Right?"

****

Kira started at Dallas's touch. It seemed sweetly possessive for a man who wasn't usually demonstrative. Glancing around the table, she caught inquisitive glances from Stormie and Jayden, and surprised looks on Gigi and Boone's faces.

"Yes, half. We're splitting the jackpot." Of course, that wasn't the truth, so she avoided Dallas's gaze.

All four of them started talking at once and she leaned closer to Dallas.

He held up a hand. "It was only fair. My money, her luck."

Kira smiled up at him. "Stupid luck."

Gigi settled in. "Tell us the whole story."

Kira and Dallas relayed the scene with a few comments from Stormie.

Their drinks arrived; three giant margaritas, three tap beers in big cowboy boot-shaped glasses, and three shots of whiskey.

The men held up their shot glasses and Jayden toasted. "To luck, stupid or otherwise."

They downed them and Kira slid her

oversized glass toward the middle of the table. "Another toast. To Gigi and Boone, lucky in love, and the reason we're all here."

The two other women slid their glasses until all three clinked, then the men tapped their boot glasses against them. The logistics of the giant cocktails had them all laughing and Gigi asked the waitress to take a couple pictures with her phone.

Stormie crossed her arms on the table and looked at Gigi. "Tell me the story of how you two met."

The loving look that passed between Gigi and Boone set Kira's heart chugging.

Dallas's hand tightened on Kira's shoulder and she looked into his dark eyes. His lips curved up just slightly and he inhaled a long breath.

The chugging in her heart increased. She wanted this man. Wanted to peel off every stitch of clothing, run her hands over the light furring on his chest, his belly, his strong thighs. She wanted to taste him, from his neck to his nipples, down his belly to his cock. To pull the hot, pulsing head into her mouth and experience the satiny texture of his tight skin, lave a salty drop of his pre-come on the tip of her tongue.

"Damn, Kira. Don't look at me like that if you don't want me to haul you over my shoulder and carry you up to our suite." His voice rumbled, quiet and sensual.

Her nipples perked as a shimmy of desire raced to her core. Placing her hand on his thigh, she grasped the hard muscle, let his heat warm her palm. "Is that a threat…or a promise."

He growled low in his chest.

"…anyway…" Gigi said sharply.

Kira and Dallas looked at her.

Gigi gave them the stink eye. "If you two are done over there, I'll finish my story."

Dallas pulled Kira closer. "We're not anywhere near done, but we'll take a break."

Kira felt heat rush to her cheeks but she grinned. "We're listening."

Boone laughed and Jayden snorted. Stormie stared at her as if she couldn't believe what she was seeing.

True, Kira had said some disparaging things to Stormie about Dallas, and her cousin had witnessed the verbal punches she and Dallas had thrown at the roulette table. But there had always been a flame burning between her and the cowboy. Kira looked at him. He was watching her. As soon as they reached their suite, that flame would become an inferno, and she welcomed the burn.

Gigi cleared her throat and spoke to Stormie. "So, together, Boone and I won the slot's progressive. Except he…" She gave Boone a loving look. "Didn't want to take half because he's such a gentleman."

Boone gave her a quick kiss. "I still don't know how she talked me into it."

Gigi wagged her brows. "I have ways of making you do what I want."

"Damn fine ways, too." His voice grew low and his arm slid across her shoulders.

Both Kira and Stormie sighed, looked at each other, then laughed.

"Chicks." Jayden made a disgusted face.

"Get used to it, brother." Boone's gaze didn't

stray from Gigi. "And learn to love it."

Gigi made a little mewing sound and touched Boone's cheek.

"So, it was perfect from then on?" Stormie's eyes were wide. "You got engaged so fast."

Boone shook his head. "No, not perfect. I screwed up real bad."

"My fault." Dallas's lips tightened into a thin line.

Dallas had sent some texts to Boone that Gigi intercepted. She gave up on Boone, gave up on love, but Boone had found a way to make it right. Thank God.

"No." Boone looked at his friend. "My fault."

"It's all in the past." Gigi waved her hand as if to erase it all. "Then, Boone took me home to his parents' ranch, he showed me the land and the house he'd inherited from his grandfather." She shrugged and smiled, her eyes bright with a sheen of moisture. "I spent a couple weeks there with him, just the two of us in that big old house. I knew that was where I wanted to be." She turned to her fiancé. "Forever."

"Forever." Boone lifted her left hand and kissed her finger where the engagement ring's big diamond twinkled brightly.

"Awww." Stormie looked a little weepy, too, and Kira felt a lump of emotion in her own throat.

"Tell her how you got engaged." Laughter filled Jayden's voice.

Chapter Three

"Oh my gosh." Kira covered her mouth with her hand to hold in the sappy sigh. "It was so romantic."

Across the booth from her and Dallas, Jayden and Stormie looked at her, smiling, but snuggled together in the back of the booth, Gigi and Boone only had grins for each other.

Dallas ran his hand up and down Kira's bare arm and goosebumps rose.

Gigi set her hand on Boone's chest. "It was romantic. A month after we met in Vegas, I flew to Maine to be with him at a rodeo. After he took first place..." Her pride showed on her face. "The band started, and he took me out on the packed dirt for a dance. I'd heard the song before, but the band was throwing in all these references to how Boone and I met. I froze."

Boone laughed. "Thought she was gonna faint." He told Stormie, "I know the guys in the band, and I asked the lead singer to tweak the song for me."

"That's so frickin' romantic." Stormie had finished over half her margarita already.

Kira should take her to the ladies' room and tell her to slow down. Kira's aunt and uncle, Stormie's parents, would kill Kira if she let her cousin get too wild. Kira was only two years older than

Stormie's twenty-two, but her cousin had grown up on a ranch, attended the local agricultural college while living at home, and hadn't had the life experiences Kira had.

"Yeah, frickin' romantic." Jayden gestured to Boone. "Tell her what you did then?"

Kira would have sworn Boone blushed under his tan. He grinned. "The band sang 'Boone has something to ask you, Gigi' and they stopped playing."

"The whole arena went silent." Gigi's voice sounded awestruck.

Boone held Gigi's hand and gazed into her eyes. "Then I went down on one knee and mumbled something about needing her, and loving her, and would she be my wife."

Gigi looked at Stormie. "I can recite the exact words." An emotionally choked laugh came from her lips. "Remind me to tell you later, at the bachelorette party. But before I have too much to drink and end up crying off all my makeup."

"I will." Stormie looked as moved as Kira felt.

"She said yes." Boone lifted Gigi's hand. "And there was this huge cheer that shook the roof. The band broke into the wedding march and I slipped the ring on her finger before she could change her mind. I grabbed this beautiful woman and took her to my hotel room." His voice went deep and trailed off as he stared at his fiancée.

She stared back, her face hot pink and her chest heaving. "Speaking of the bachelorette party. We'd better get going. The Hummers will be in front of the hotel in a couple hours." They'd rented two stretch Hummer limos, one in white for the women, and one in black for the guys.

Kira could tell what Gigi and Boone would be doing in their suite for the next two hours. "You two go, have some time together before we pull you apart, and utterly embarrass the hell out of each of you in public."

"Don't wear him out, Gigi." Jayden stood, helping Stormie from the booth to let the engaged couple out. "Us cowboys have big plans for him tonight."

Gigi giggled as she and Boone slid out of the booth. "I'll try not to." They left so fast, they were nearly running.

"While we're up…" Jayden laid his hand on Stormie's back. "Wanna go see if we can win a jackpot of our own?"

Oh heck, no. Kira had to stop this. "Ah, maybe we should—"

Stormie grinned at Jayden. "Okay. Let's go."

"Stormie." Kira moved to get up and Dallas tugged her back down. "They'll be okay."

The two walked out of the bar, Jayden's hand resting on Stormie's back.

Dallas pulled out his phone. "I'll send Jay a reminder." He started typing. "Better yet, a threat."

"Thank you." She felt a little guilty letting her cousin loose with a rodeo cowboy, but when Dallas put his phone away then looked at her with those sexy eyes, only one thought crowded her mind. Naked.

"Wanna go check out our suite?" His face softened and his eyes lured her.

"Okay." She swallowed. Not her most brilliant or sexy line, but her body tingled with desire.

He charged the drinks to the credit balance on their comped suite and led her to the elevators. He pressed the up button and tugged her against him, pressing her breasts against his hard chest, and her hips against his granite erection.

"Kira, I want you. I've wanted you since Christmas." He let out a long breath. "Are you gonna want to talk first? Get everything settled between us...I mean, the shit that happened in December?"

Could she wait that long to have him kissing her? Touching her? Sliding his shaft deep inside her?

They'd had a fierce argument in the hotel's lobby bar, she'd accused him, he'd been both insulted and angry. It had been a scene she'd regretted ever since.

The elevator opened and they jumped in, pressed the top button, and found themselves enclosed and alone together.

"Just tell me one thing, Dallas." This would either piss him off and send him stomping, or it would clear the way for her to let the sexy charge between them amp up.

He stiffened. "Okay. Ask me." He had to know what was coming next.

"Did you abuse your girlfriend?" Kira held her breath.

Dallas's eyes sobered as he locked gazes with hers. "Kira, I swear on my mother's grave, I have never hit a woman, a child, or an animal. I can explain the assault charges, but it'll take a while."

She believed him. Based on his words, on what she knew from the short time they'd spent together, and from the few things Boone had told her without breaking his promise of confidentiality to

Dallas. He was not guilty.

She slid her palms up his chest and locked her fingers around the back of his neck. "Action first. Talk later."

His eyes glowed, half lidded, and his breath blew hot on her face. "Damn."

****

Dallas couldn't hold back the growl that rumbled out of him as he tugged Kira against him, one hand on her back, the other cupping her tight, round ass. "Sweetheart, you may not be in any shape to talk after the action." Tipping his head, he took her mouth with his. Her lips pressed soft and warm against his as they finally shared their first kiss.

His belly quivered with the raw desire to take this woman hot, rough, and fast. His tongue invaded her mouth, the sweetness of her margarita lingered and mixed with the sensual taste of her.

The elevator doors slid apart and he flung out a hand to hold them open. He ended the kiss but she clung to him with her eyes closed. "Just a few more feet, sweetheart."

Her lids rose slowly. "If I'd known you kissed like that…" She sucked in a choppy breath.

He grinned and scooped her up in his arms. "We woulda been doing this since December?" Ah, shit, that sounded like he was looking for something long term with her. He strode down the hall looking for their suite.

A little pucker marred the perfect skin between her brows. "Do you think we can make up for lost time?" She gave him a wicked leer.

A chuckle rolled from his chest as he set her

down in front of the Wrangler Suite. "Damn sure gonna try."

He slid the keycard from his pocket and opened the door, guiding her in ahead of him.

"Oh. This is gorgeous." Kira walked in, looking down at the pure white carpet.

Dallas followed, taking her hand and leading her to the black leather couch, bracketed by two red leather chairs. The furniture faced floor-to-ceiling windows that glowed with the setting sun behind the skyline of Vegas. "Fancy."

He looked to his right. A small wooden bar with two stools stood in front of a mural of wild mustangs racing across scrubland.

"Perfect choice of suites." Kira let go of his hand and walked to the bar. A silver bucket held a bottle of chilling champagne. She tapped it with her finger. "Should we?"

He shook his head. Behind her, the open door to the bedroom showed the room radiating in golden sunlight. He gestured toward it. "Should we…check out the bedroom first?"

She glanced toward the room and looked back at him, her lips parted, her nipples hard against her soft dress, and her cheeks warmed with color. "Turn off your phone." She backed into the bedroom and pulled her phone from the little white bag hanging from her shoulder.

He tugged his phone from his pocket, turned it to silent, and tossed it onto the bar. Blood rushed from his head down to his groin, filling his cock and pulsing in his balls. Following her into the bedroom, he barely glanced at the big window framing the view of the strip, the red satin bedspread, or heavy wood furniture before his gaze riveted on her.

Kira faced him and kicked off her sandals.

He mirrored her, toeing off his boots. Somehow, a barefoot Kira wound him up faster than any other woman had, barefoot, or butt naked. He had to watch this connection they had. It could last a few days, even a week 'til after Boone's wedding. But that would be the end. No long-term, long-distance anything.

But for now, this was good. She was as hot and ready as he was, and he couldn't deny himself a taste of Kira.

She sauntered over toward him, the look on her face seductive and impatient. She lifted his hat from his head and set it on the dresser. She must appreciate the importance of a cowboy's best hat. Tugging at the first button of his shirt, she darted her tongue across her bottom lip. "How do you like it, cowboy?"

His hips jerked as a blast of lust rocketed into his shaft. "Hard and fast the first time, sweetheart. Then slow. Hours of sweaty, hot sex in a dozen different positions."

Her eyelids fluttered as she sucked in a breath. "Somehow, I knew you'd want it just like that."

He unfastened the six small buttons at the front of her dress. "And you're okay with skipping the party tonight?" Boone would understand, based on basic guy code, but Gigi? He doubted it.

She slowly shook her head. "She'd kill me." She tugged his shirt out of his pants and finished the last buttons.

"More likely, she'd send Boone up here to get

you, and no matter what you said, I'd be the bad guy." He slid one dress strap off her shoulder revealing a lacy blue bra strap. His big, tanned hand against her pale skin revealed her fragile side. It caught him by surprise and shook him a little.

"Okay, let's do this." She ran her hands up his abs to his chest and purred for a second. "Let's do the hard and fast thing and see what else we have time for, after."

He slid his fingers across her shoulder. Soft, delicate. His palm eased down to her bicep and he took her whole arm in his hand, his fingers and thumb touching. "You're so…slight." He would need to be careful with her, and not lose himself when he wanted to get rough.

Her fingers played in his chest hair. "I fool people. I'm loud and assertive, and they don't realize I'm kinda skinny."

He looked into her eyes. "You're not skinny. You're…" What had his mom called it? "Willowy."

Her brows rose. "That's probably the nicest thing you've ever said to me, cowboy."

Damn, she was right. He hadn't been very forthcoming with his compliments. "I've got a few other lines that you'll find much nicer." He tugged off his shirt and threw it.

"Oh, uh huh." She touched him, his shoulders, his abs, his chest, his arms. "You are packed, big guy."

He flexed a little. "Helps me hang on to whatever I'm ridin'."

She lifted a brow and gave him a skeptical look.

He laughed. "Sorry, that sounded a hell of a

lot better in my head than it did comin' out my mouth."

"Try again." She smiled as she unbuckled his belt.

The brush of her fingers sent wicked flares down his belly to tighten his gut and tingle at the base of his spine.

"I'm gonna peel this dress off you." With one finger of each hand, he eased the dress straps down and did what he'd promised.

As the garment slid past her beautiful breasts, his mouth watered at the hard, peachy nipples peeking at him from under the lace of her bra.

She shivered and her lips formed a small "O."

"I'll suck those perfect nipples into my mouth and play with them until you rip your nails down my back."

Kira swallowed. "Yes, I can do that." Her voice came out on a breath.

He lowered her dress to the slight swell of her hips where it caught on her panties in back, hung up where her sweet ass rounded perfectly.

With a shimmy, she shook it loose and let it drop.

"Aw God." Her body glowed in the setting sun. Long, thin legs, a flat stomach boasting an outie belly button that he had to taste. Her panties matched her bra, blue and lacy. Her ribs showed slightly in a very feminine display that drew him forward for a touch.

She blinked rapidly, her mouth opened as her breathing sped up.

The first touch of his fingertips on her skin

jolted them both, sending a bolt of desire down into his gut. He eased his palm along her ribs and stepped behind her. He ran his knuckles down her spine, stopping when he reached the elastic of her panties.

"You can tear them off," she whispered.

"Uh uh." He hooked his finger under the band. "You'd make me pay for them out of my half." Catching the label embroidered into the back, he recognized the brand from his favorite TV commercials. "And I bet these are damned expensive drawers."

She laughed. "Drawers?" Then she shivered. "It'd be worth losing my favorite drawers to get you moving faster."

"Gettin' kinda bossy, there, Kira." He grasped her hips. "This is the part of our evening where I go as slow as I please. And I want to enjoy every second of unwrapping you."

A little mewl escaped her lips. "Tease."

"Yep." He sat on his heels. "Nothin' for you to do but relax and enjoy it." He caught the sides of her panties, careful not to snag them with his rough hands. Easing them down slowly, he revealed her fine, firm ass...and a tiny tattoo. "What's this? A little surprise for me?" It looked like a bunch of colored circles.

Chapter Four

Dallas sat on his heels on the plush bedroom carpeting with Kira standing in front of him, facing away. She arched her back and tipped her ass in a mouthwatering display. "Balloons."

He turned her a few inches until the sun caught the ink on her ass cheek. "I'll be damned."

"I've always loved them. Still do." She straightened up. "Kind of silly, huh?"

He kissed the spot, a slow brush of his lips and a decadent flick of his tongue. Her taste, sweet and salty, burst on his tongue. "Not silly at all." If he had to get a tattoo of something he loved, would it be bronc riding? A sexy buckle bunny? Hell no. He'd have Kira's whole gorgeous body tattooed on him. Pulling back, he frowned. Had he used the word "love" in context with this woman? His warning bells went off, sounding like the words "don't trust" as they rang in his ears.

"Dallas? Everything okay?" She stiffened. "Oh cripes, are you a tattoo hater?"

He chuckled. "No, I'm not a tattoo hater." He shook off the fear that threatened to end his enjoyment of a wild, no-expectations night—or week—with the hottest woman he'd ever known. "I'm just taking my time." After sliding her panties down to her ankles, he ran his hands up her legs.

She shivered and leaned back a little.

"Too rough?" His calluses were permanent, from years of working with horses.

"Nu uh," she breathed. "Feels really good."

Did she like it a little rough?

He wrapped both hands around one thigh and his thumbs overlapped. So thin. "God, I love your thighs." Delicate, translucent skin. He had to take it slow, choose positions that wouldn't bang her around and bruise her.

"You're a thigh man?"

A short laugh barked from his chest. "Not until just this second." He gently grasped her legs in his hands, feeling her muscles quiver.

She stepped one foot out of her panties and spread her legs a few inches wider. "Take your time." Her voice sounded frustrated. "It's not like I'm dying for release here."

With a grin, he bit her ass cheek, the one without the tattoo. "Sarcasm will only delay things." He rubbed his thumbs along the backs of her thighs, right under where they met her ass. Unable to resist, he licked the same spot, long, sweeping drags of his tongue starting from the outside and ending at her ass crack.

The scent of her arousal, musky and sweet, invaded his nose, stabbing through his brain and sending slices of lust down his spine. He nibbled on her ass cheeks as she moaned and clenched her hands into fists.

With quick nips and licks along the cleft of her ass, he stood. He pressed kisses to each of her vertebrae, soaking in her floral scent. When he reached her bra, he unhooked it with one hand, a technique he and Boone had practiced and perfected when they were teens.

Wrapping his arms around her waist, he pressed his hands to her stomach and snugged the length of his denim-clad erection against her firm ass.

"I want you, woman."

She dropped her head back onto his shoulder and placed her hands over his.

The gesture struck an extra heartbeat in his chest. He liked having her in his arms. It felt like…home. Home? Goddamnit, where had that come from? He barely resisted jumping back. And running. Sex. This was sex and nothing more. He couldn't afford any more.

She turned to face him and one bra strap slid off her shoulder.

Sex was easy to lose himself in. He focused on her blushing cheeks and dilated pupils that made her eyes a dark green. "You're beautiful, Kira. I'm a lucky man."

Her lips curved up. "You are, and I hope I'll be getting lucky pretty quick here, too."

He waggled his brows at her. "Pretty quick. Still a passel of teasing left to do."

"Uhhh."

In his arms, her body vibrated with need. He pulled her bra straps down and tossed the lacy thing onto a chair in the corner. "Damn." Perfect D cups, so pale he could see small veins under the surface. Her nipples and darker areolas puckered tighter at his stare.

"Are you a breast man, too?"

He held her breasts in his palms, loving the

softness of her skin over the firm orbs. His thumbs flicked her tight nipples. "Yep. Breasts, thighs, ass. Every amazing part of you that I can't get enough of."

Her body shimmied with each pass of his thumbs. "I have a couple parts…" She sucked in a breath. "That you haven't seen yet."

His balls heated and another burst of blood flooded his cock. "I want to explore you, spend long hours tasting and touching."

"Mmmm. We don't have that long."

He laced his fingers through her satiny hair. "You are the most impatient…" He tilted her head and kissed her, his lips parting hers, his tongue running along her teeth, fencing with her tongue until the pressure in his groin nearly made him black out.

With his face an inch from hers, he nipped at her lip. "Look at me."

Slowly, her lids rose halfway.

"I'm going to use my mouth on your pussy, Kira. I'm going to lick and suck you until you come for me, come all over my face."

Her mouth parted as she dragged in air.

He wanted that mouth, those full, perfect lips around his cock. But he'd save that treat for later, after they came back from the parties. They'd indulge in a long, wild night of sex. A dozen positions flashed through his mind.

"Then I want to slide my cock into your slick pussy, slow and easy until you take it all, and my balls rub up against your ass." He pinched her nipples, tweaking them into swollen buds.

She grasped his shoulders as her knees wobbled.

He held her hips and knelt before her. "Aw

sweetheart, you left a little patch of your curly red hair for me to play in." He kissed her just above the tuft, and it tickled his chin. "How did you know I like a little muff?"

"I'm a mind reader." She ran her fingers through his hair.

"I am, too. Right now…" He looked up at her and lapped at her mound. "I can tell you want to grab my hair and pull me into your pussy."

She fisted her hands in his hair. "Would it do any good?" She tugged lightly. "You seem to want to torture me instead of please me."

"I am a mean bastard, but when you climax higher than you ever have before, you'll thank me." He rubbed his face in her soft, trimmed hair and glanced up at her.

"You talk a good fuck, but I need you to prove it."

His hips slammed forward at the nasty word coming out of her sweet mouth. A lady, an angel, but with a little bit of devil poking its way out just for him.

Grabbing her wrist, he pulled her off balance as he stood, and caught her up in his arms. "Comin' right up, ma'am."

She kissed his shoulder. "Gotta get you naked, first."

Her sweet gesture made his belly flutter. He walked to the far side of the bed, furthest from the window. He didn't want anyone to see her, but she was so beautiful in the sunlight, he hated to close the curtains. He laid her gently on the mattress.

Kira's hair fanned around her head. Against

the red comforter, her pale skin glowed with life. She ran her hands on the satin then writhed her body over it. "Slippery. This will be fun."

He unbuttoned his jeans, unzipped, and tugged them off, along with his socks.

"Tightie whities? Really?" She stared at where his cock tented the briefs.

"Gotta keep everything in control." It struck him that his underwear was a metaphor for his life.

"Time to lose control, Dallas." She propped up on her elbows and gestured toward his groin. "And time to lose those drawers." She licked her lips, deliberately teasing him. "Take it off, cowboy, and let loose of your epic restraint."

Was he that easy to read? That was what he'd become over the years, and even more so since Layna's betrayal. "How's this for no restraint?" He turned his back to her. The sun pouring in the window warmed his back and highlighted him like he was on stage. His shadow loomed large on the wall in front of him. He lifted his arms and flexed.

"Oh yes, big guy." Her voice purred low and sexy. "Give me something to dream about."

He grabbed the sides of his underwear and flexed again, concentrating on his back muscles.

"Damn, cowboy! You should be doing this on stage."

"Ha." He could loosen up a bit in front of her. In public? It'd scare the shit out of him. "This is a private show, for one…" He leered at her over his shoulder. "…lucky lady."

"Oh baby, do it."

He slowly peeled his drawers down his ass, letting them catch under it, showcasing it for her.

"Sweet ass. Shake it for me."

"Shake it?" He shrugged. "I wouldn't know how to begin to do that."

She laughed. "Wiggle it then? Please?"

"For you, sweetheart, I'll try." He jerked his hips side to side, then found a circular rhythm, one that he'd like to use with his cock deep inside Kira's hot pussy. His head leaked a drop of pre-cum.

"Cowboy, I'm going to be thinking of this tonight when the girls and I are at the strip club. Nobody will compare to you."

Time to stop fucking around and get down to it. He pulled off his underwear, turned, and flashed her a full hard-on as he flexed his muscles.

Her gaze zoomed to his stiff cock. The drop of natural lube glistened in the sun. She sat up then crawled across the bed to him, her eyes feral, her tongue tracing her lips.

Heat bloomed at the base of his spine and every male part around it started tingling. He stepped closer to the bed.

With her face an inch from the tip of his cock, she stopped. "You're so big, Dallas. Thick and long." She looked up at him. "I want this in my mouth. In my pussy. Between my tits. And in my ass."

Flares shot up his spine and popped off in his head. He grabbed her hair and tipped her head back. "Taste me."

Her lips curved into a wicked smile as she shifted closer and took his head into her mouth, licking his slit.

His ass tightened, his balls contracted, and with one more flick of her tongue, he'd be gone. He pulled back. "Sweetheart, you don't know how close I am, how desperate you make me." Dallas eased her back onto the comforter. "But this cowboy's a gentleman, and it's 'ladies first'."

She wiggled and shivered. "I like the sound of that." She lay on the bed, a temptation he couldn't resist.

He lay perpendicular to her, his head at her hip. His palm made circles on her thigh. "All I can think of is these gorgeous legs wrapped around my head."

"Mmmm." She arched her back. "Please."

He liked it when she begged. Rolling her onto her side away from him, he kissed her tattoo, licked the seam of her ass, and lifted her leg. Nuzzling his way between her legs, he lowered her leg.

Her thighs pressed on each side of his head, cutting off all sense of hearing. He grasped her legs, holding her there. He licked the tender flesh of her inner thighs, the taste of her skin melding with the juices of her arousal.

"Sweet, like honey." He ran his tongue along the soft, peachy lips of her pussy. "I could stay here forever."

****

Kira's brain fuzzed and dimmed. Her sexy cowboy with his head between her legs had already stoked her so high and hot, she could come with his next lick. She'd never experienced anything as tender and sensual as Dallas's seduction.

Lying on her side, she looked down and forced her eyes open. The dimming in her head was due to the sun dropping below the mountains, but the fuzzing was all him.

His dark head lay on her thigh, his short hair soft against her skin. His hands on her legs held her where he wanted her as his lips created magic that pulsed in her core and flooded her pussy.

"God, you taste good." His muffled voice reached her as he sucked her swollen folds into his mouth.

Reaching down with one hand, Kira tunneled her fingers through his hair. Her breathing sped and her hips and ass tightened. Tingles of pleasure raced through her belly and climbed her spine to batter at the precarious control she held over her looming orgasm.

He shifted and his tongue plunged into her slit, fucking her in a slow rhythm that started her shaking.

"Dallas, I'm close."

"Sweetheart, hang on. I haven't eaten my fill yet."

She dropped her head back and concentrated on holding off, centering her thoughts on his talented mouth.

Placing hot, open-mouthed kisses on her pussy lips, he touched her everywhere he could reach. Her thighs, her mound, then, finally, her clit. His lips sucked her bud, gently at first, then he nipped it between his teeth and set his tongue fluttering quickly, ingenious little flicks that sent a bolt of heat racing up her spine to blow her control to pieces and send her spinning wildly into a manic orgasm.

He held her bucking hips as she left her body and twisted through waves of pleasure so intense, she couldn't catch her breath. Darkness engulfed her, punctuated by lightning streaks of delight as his tongue worked faster, sending her deeper.

Another orgasm ricocheted through her, making her scream with bliss. She reached complete weightlessness and slowly descended, returning to her body, regaining her brain function, and quivering down low where Dallas softly kissed her and lapped up her juices.

"Sweetheart. Nothing has ever been so right."

"So good," she managed to pant. Twin orgasms that shook her, body and soul. Could she survive the orgasms he'd give her with his cock pounding deep into her?

He lifted her leg, left the bed, and within seconds spooned himself behind her, holding her tight, kissing her ear, her neck, and whispering gentle words. His cock lay hard and hot against her ass.

"Dallas." She forced open her eyes to see the spectacular colors of the sunset over the twinkling lights of Vegas. "You were brilliant."

He chuckled, and the vibration worked its way into her. "Glad I pleased you, ma'am." He nibbled her shoulder. "Twice, if my accounting is correct."

A lazy smile curved her mouth and she turned to look at him.

In the evocative lighting, his eyes shone, dark and passionate.

He kissed her, filling her with the taste of beer and whiskey combined with his natural spiciness and the lingering taste of her own juices. His scent invaded her and she breathed deeply of musky male.

Her nipples puckered and a chill raced along her spine. She wanted more. Wanted all of him, inside her, on top of her, taking her, taking what he wanted from her.

"Kira." He whispered the words against her lips. "Let me make love to you."

Her chest froze, her heart sped. Not fuck. Make love. "Yes. Take me, Dallas." She could feel herself sliding in too deep. Did she care? She'd never really been in love. This could be her chance to experience what Gigi called "the best feeling she could ever imagine."

He rolled on top of her, pressing her down into the comforter. "Am I too heavy?"

His concern warmed her. "No. You feel...perfect."

Rearing up a little, he lifted a brow. "No one's ever called me perfect before. You sure you're in your right mind?"

"Uh, I really don't know where my head is at right now." She cupped his cheeks in her palms. "But I don't want to let this mood go." Pulling up, she pressed a quick kiss to his lips. "Got a condom?"

He grinned and showed her his right hand. "Yep." Ripping the packet with his teeth, he opened it then rolled the latex onto his big shaft. He moved up, using his thighs to spread her legs.

Dropping back on the bed, she grasped his biceps. "I need you inside me."

With a groan, he cupped her pussy and slid one finger into her opening. "You're wet and hot and I don't want to wait another second."

"Then don't."

"Kira." He waited until she focused on him. "If I get too rough, if anything hurts, you yell 'stop' and I will."

Her chest ached with the thought of his concern for her. "I think I'd like it rough, cowboy." She reached down and grabbed his cock.

It pulsed in her hand and he jerked his hips forward.

Guiding the hard shaft to her pussy, she lifted her hips from the bed, filling herself with the big head of his cock.

"Damn, Kira." His voice shook. "Give a guy a break."

Chapter Five

Kira smiled at the power she held over him. "No." She lay back on the bed, looking up at him with eyes that blurred with her rising lust. She wasn't giving Dallas any chance to slow down.

He shook his head once, twice, then his gaze locked with hers as he slid his thick staff deep inside her.

The feeling of fullness burned through her, tightening her core and throbbing in her tender clit. "Feels so good." Had she said it aloud or just in her head?

"You're..." His head dropped as he withdrew and pushed back in again. "So fucking tight."

She clenched around him, closing her eyes to absorb every sensation.

"Aw hell." He pulled back and slammed into her. "I'm gonna embarrass myself, but sweetheart, when you do that little thing you just did, I know I won't last the full eight seconds."

A surprised laugh escaped her chest.

He narrowed his eyes. "I wanted this to go a while. But you're too damn hot."

"Ride me, cowboy. This time, fast and wild. Next time, slow and sweet."

"I promise. Next time...hours and hours." Moving up to kneel between her legs, he planted one hand on the bed above her shoulder, grabbed her leg, and lifted it, holding it in the crook of his arm. "Can't hold back, Kira. You're so fucking sexy."

The new position, the angle of his cock, let him drive into her deeper. Beads of sweat formed on his brow. His hips worked, pumping his thick cock into her, dragging it out and pushing in again. Each stroke grazed against her g-spot.

Grabbing fistfuls of comforter, she let herself slide into the fog that promised another unruly orgasm.

He grunted and moaned her name as he pistoned into her, her body held in place only by his arm at her shoulder.

"I like it rough." She panted the words as her vision went white, her hearing faded, and rushing sensations shimmied up her body from her core.

Dallas moved faster, pumped into her harder, his groans becoming louder until he shouted, "Fuck, Kira, take it, take all of me."

She exploded into darkness, knowing only the hard banging of Dallas's hips against hers, the joy of her climax echoing through her, and the sure knowledge that her cowboy could have her, body and soul, if he wanted her.

With two final pumps, Dallas nose-dived into the comforter beside her, then rolled, taking her with him to lie on top of him.

His breath panted from his chest, his heart beat rapidly, and his forehead shone with sweat.

She kissed the spot over his heart. She could lie here forever.

"Aw jeez, sweetheart, I'm sorry."

She lifted her head and looked into his dark

eyes. "Sorry?"

"I didn't mean to be so rough."

Digging her nails into his chest, she made her smile sensual. "Cowboy, it was perfect. I like it when you're unleashed."

"You do, huh?" He grinned. "Kira, sweetheart, when we have sex, there'll be very few times when I'm on the leash."

"Good." She imagined him taking her from behind, or in the shower, or against a wall, or making her ride him hard and fast. "You're a fantasy come true."

With a groan, he pulled her in for a kiss. He possessed her, his tongue twining with hers, tasting her then sucking her tongue into his mouth where he captured it with his lips. He slowed the kiss when his cock hardened against her belly. "We've gotta get ready, don't we."

She checked the clock radio. "Half an hour. Figure fifteen minutes for a shower and makeup."

He traced her cheek with one finger. "You don't wear any makeup."

She batted her mascara-enhanced lashes. "Nature didn't give me these thick, black lashes, you know."

"Mm. Okay. So, that leaves us with fifteen minutes." He poked his hard shaft into her hip. "What should we do?"

Although she wanted desperately to repeat everything they just did, there was something hanging over them that she wanted to clear away. She made a face. "Can we talk?"

He dropped his head and threw his arms out to

the side. "Words designed to soften any erection."

She laughed and smacked his chest. "Better to do it now than when we get back from the party tomorrow morning."

"True." He eased out from under her. "Hang on a second." He headed to the bathroom.

Kira stretched, feeling sore muscles and tingly flesh, but loving every twinge and ache because it came from Dallas making unleashed love to her.

She piled pillows up at the headboard and pulled back the comforter, climbing under the sheet. This conversation would be less awkward without nudity.

Dallas came out of the bathroom and pulled on his underwear. "Water?"

She nodded, he headed into the next room and came back with two ice cold bottles. Sitting back on the pillows next to her, he sighed. "Want me to start?"

"Yes, please." She touched his arm. "But tell me only what you feel comfortable sharing."

"All right." He picked at the label of his water bottle. "It was last summer, August, I think. I met Layna at a rodeo in northern California. We spent the night." He looked at her then glanced away. "I stayed the week. We hit it off. She came back with me to Reno."

He'd fallen hard and fast. It didn't seem like the Dallas she knew.

"After a few months, she hadn't found a job, and wanted access to my bank accounts, saying she wanted to take care of things around the apartment when I was on the road." He took a long pull of water. "When I said no, we argued."

Kira's nerves jangled. She could see where

this was headed.

"Sometimes…" He looked at her, his eyes full of sorrow. "I'd come home and she'd have bruises."

She reached out but drew her hand back. She wanted so badly to comfort him, but he needed to get this out.

"She explained that she was a klutz, and that she wanted to join the gym, but I wouldn't give her access to my accounts, so she couldn't." He smacked the bottle on his bare thigh. "I offered to set up automatic payments, and I gave her cash, lots of cash, enough to buy food and clothes and whatever else she needed. But she was angry that I didn't trust her with my account information."

He went silent for so long, she thought he might not be able to say any more.

Dallas hauled in a breath. "Around Thanksgiving, I knew it was over. I asked her to move out. Offered to pay for her gas back to California and a couple month's rent and expenses."

He stood and walked to the window. "She started shaking, begged me to reconsider. When I held her and told her we were through, she picked up her keys and looked at me. Her eyes were dead, lifeless. She said, 'You give me no choice, Dallas,' and she walked out."

"No choice?"

His head turned and he faced her. "I didn't know what it meant until the trial."

****

Every muscle, every bone in Dallas's body hurt as he told Kira the story of his last girlfriend. The last woman he'd made love to, the last woman he'd trusted—who made him the hollow shell he was today.

Kira sat up in bed and crossed her legs under the sheet, keeping it tucked firmly around her. "Until the trial? But that wasn't until last month."

He crossed his arms over his bare chest. "How did you know about that?" He barely held back his anger.

Her eyes opened wide.

"Your investigator, right?"

"Dallas, honestly, I didn't ask him to keep track of you." She reached out a hand. "Please. Come and sit."

He let go of the distrust that gut punched him at the smallest sign of a lie. Trudging over to her, he sat on the edge of the bed.

She dropped her hand. "He called me." She shook her head. "His contact in Reno let him know the results of the trial, and he thought I'd want to know." Clasping her hands in her lap, she started to speak a few times, before she said, "I'm sorry."

"It's okay. I'm guessing you wouldn't have come up to this suite with me if he hadn't told you I was innocent."

"Well, Boone had mentioned..." She pressed her lips together as if she'd let out a secret.

"Boone told you?"

She nodded. "I'd go with Gigi sometimes to rodeos. And he came to New York a couple times." She scooted closer to him. "He didn't tell me anything except you were found not guilty, and that he knew you too well to ever believe you could harm a woman."

Dallas laid his hand on top of hers on her

knee. "I'm not pissed, so you can stop looking at me like I'm a bomb about to go off."

Her eyes held a wounded look. "You have a history of that with me, you know."

He mentally kicked himself. "Yep, and I've been regretting it since Christmas."

"All forgiven." She waved a hand through the air as if by magic it could be forgotten as well.

"Thanks, Kira." He looked at her closely. She was a woman he could easily become attached to. "You're good for me."

Her cheeks colored attractively, but she didn't speak.

"Anyway, a couple days after Thanksgiving, I'd just gotten home from a rodeo, and Layna showed up. Just walked in the apartment. Except…she was battered. Her eyes were blackened, lip split, nose bleeding. Her arms were black and blue." His heart beat faster remembering his fear. "I asked her what happened, but she wouldn't talk for a few minutes. Then she gave me the threat."

Kira's fingers pressed to her mouth. Her eyes stared, wide and frightened.

"She said I could either give her the twenty eight thousand dollars I had in my bank account, or she'd tell the police I'd beaten her."

"Oh shit. Oh God, Dallas. You must have been just sick."

"Sick? Yeah. I'd let her into my life. I'd trusted her. I…loved her. And the whole time, it was the money." He had to hold Kira. Dallas sat back against the headboard, lifted her in between his legs, tucking her head under his chin.

She snuggled in with a quick kiss to his collarbone.

His heart went from aching from the fear caused by reliving that day, to the sweet pleasure of holding this amazing woman close.

"I couldn't let her get away with it, Kira. It wasn't the money, it was the idea that she and whoever was making her do this, whoever had beaten her, couldn't be allowed to do this to someone else."

"You did the right thing."

"Did I?" A humorless laugh echoed in the room. "She'd already called the police from her cell phone just outside the apartment door. They arrived in minutes and cuffed me. Hauled me out of there. My neighbors saw it. Saw her standing there beaten and bleeding…" He held his breath to regain composure.

Kira sniffled and he felt moisture run down his chest.

The thought of her crying over him…fuck, he was so screwed. How was he supposed to let her go after the wedding next week? How had he let himself grow so close to her?

"They took her to the hospital, and me to jail. They didn't find her blood or DNA on my hands, but I had cuts and bruising from the rodeo. Based on this and her complaint, I was booked. It was nearly morning before Boone and his dad bailed me out."

"I'm so sorry. It must have been horrible."

"It wasn't so bad. It surprised me how I never felt fear. I knew I'd be exonerated."

She looked up at him. "You're a strong man, Dallas. I'm proud that you did what was right."

He brushed a tear off her cheek. "Plus, I

learned a whole passel of swell new legal terms."

She laughed softly and tucked back into him. "Cowboy." It was all she said, but the one word carried a whole chapter of meaning.

"My neighbors wanted the building owner to evict me, but I fought that, too. The town and county newspapers carried the story, and the rodeo association heard about it. I had to appeal suspension of my association membership pending the outcome of the trial."

"She really disrupted your life. Do you ever wish you'd just paid her?"

"I did a couple of times…a couple hundred times. But I had to see it through." He stared out the window at the flashing lights of the strip. "At the trial, my lawyer, who had been a friend of my parents, represented me pro-bono… Another big law word."

She laughed quietly. "That's nice of him. He must have believed in you."

"He did." Besides Boone, Jayden, and their family, he was the only person who'd stood by him, and didn't treat him like a criminal. "He argued that there was no physical evidence; on me, on her, or in the apartment, to prove that there had been an altercation. He noted that one of the police responders had checked her car and found the hood hot, like it had just been driven. And she'd said I kept her locked in the apartment with me for an hour while I…hit her."

"Oh Dallas." She shivered then took a breath. "That was good police work."

"Lucky. Stupid luck, again."

She sat back. "Take your luck any way you

can get it."

Staring into her beautiful green eyes, he thanked luck for bringing Kira to him, not once, but twice. "I will, from now on." He took her hand. "The lawyer was good. He found evidence of her being hospitalized a few times for what looked like abuse. These happened before I met her."

"So, whatever man, or woman, she was with had her under their control. Made her do these things for money."

"I'm pretty sure it was a man." The thought of Layna cheating on him was almost as agonizing as thinking of her being abused all those years. "Two of the neighbors in the building had seen her with a man. They testified for me."

"You got your life back." She tried a smile.

He shook his head. "My physical life, but not my quality of life."

"What do you mean?"

"She stole from me." His faith in people, his ability to trust, and possibly even his ability to love again. Love and trust were too closely bound.

"What did she take?"

Dallas wasn't going to go anywhere near his emotional issues while Kira was in his arms. "While I was in jail, she went through the apartment and took all my championship belt buckles."

"Oh no."

"It was really all I had of value. I didn't realize they were gone until a week later. By then, she'd pawned them all over Reno. It took me a month to find all of them. Well, all except one." He could still see the shiny face of that buckle. "My favorite. Grand champion."

"I know how impressive that is, now that Gigi's hanging out with a rodeo man. Can't you get it replaced?"

He shook his head. "Nope. They made only one. I won it a year to the date after my parents died, and I dedicated it to them that night."

"Dallas, that's so sad." Her eyes glittered again.

"Don't worry. It's just a buckle."

"It's more than that." She rubbed his cheek. "It's your life as you knew it."

"That's shot to shit, Kira. Ain't never gonna be the same again. I gotta learn to live with what I have left."

She tipped her head. "It'll take a while to heal. Have you thought about pro—"

"Professional help?" He swung his leg high over her head and got off the bed. "Now you're sounding like Gigi." He padded into the bathroom.

"I guess we're done talking?" she called from the bedroom.

"Look at the clock." He turned on the shower, waiting for it to get hot.

Squealing, Kira ran in, tucked her hair up in the hotel-provided shower cap, and jumped into the icy stream of water. "Five minutes, cowboy. And if you're not ready, I'm leaving without you!"

He laughed and jumped in with her, damn near freezing his nuts off.

Chapter Six

At eight fifteen, Dallas held open the casino's front door and let Kira walk ahead of him out onto the sidewalk. The dry desert heat hit him. He inhaled, enjoying real air after all the canned air conditioning inside the building.

They were the last to arrive. Boone and Gigi stood off to the side, held tightly in each other's arms, talking.

Jayden stood talking to a couple of rodeo buddies, Rance and Mitch. Three of Boone's friends, Ace, Toby, and Bryan hung out by the black stretch Hummer, looking ready to get going. Ace worked on Boone's parents' farm, and Toby and Bryan owned small ranches adjacent to Boone's land.

Stormie slid out of the back door of the white Hummer. "She's here! Let's go!"

Everyone turned to look at Kira and Dallas.

At their stares, he almost dropped his hand from her back, but he stood firm. He knew he'd get shit from Jayden and Boone, maybe even from Gigi and Stormie, but he wanted to show them that Kira was his woman. For right now, anyway.

He whispered in her ear, "See you soon, sexy."

She turned her face toward him and he stole a kiss.

"Oh man." Jayden crossed his arms over his chest. "Stop with the mushy stuff and let's get partying."

Dallas tugged Kira tighter. "It's Valentine's Day tomorrow. Mushy is good."

Kira laughed and slid out of his grasp. "See you soon, big guy."

The women climbed into their Hummer and headed north. The men piled in theirs and headed south. They ate steak dinners in a reserved party room at one of the casinos on the strip, then headed to two other casinos for drinks in the bars.

At one bar, Boone sent Dallas the picture of all six of them at the Roundup Bar earlier that day toasting with their giant drinks. Dallas saved the picture and stared a few minutes at Kira's expression. God, she was pretty. Boone took the opportunity to bring up Gigi's concerns about Kira, but said he only poked his nose in Dallas's business because the boss told him to.

Dallas had no response, and they let it drop. Boone was used to his silences, and knew that it didn't mean Dallas wasn't listening.

Around midnight, the men arrived at the strip club.

The girls' Hummer was already there. The building had two levels, the female exotic dancers worked the lower level, and the males worked the top floor.

In the dark room, lights flashed where the women danced on the stage. The cowboys slipped into their reserved booth, which had a pole centered in the middle of the table. "Hello, happiness." Rance hauled out his wallet and ordered the well-primed cowboys a round of longnecks and whiskey shots.

Jayden took out his own wallet and set a small stack of twenties in front of Boone. "Dad told me to make sure you have a good time tonight."

Boone shook his head. They'd positioned him at the end of the booth. "I'll let you buy me one lap dance, but I'm not gonna be—"

"Bullshit." Rance stood, placed his finger and thumb into his mouth, and whistled loudly.

A couple of the girls noticed them and wandered over, big smiles on their faces.

Dallas hid his grin. Rance was a wild one, a bull rider gaining on Boone in the rankings. With his green eyes, black hair, and loud personality, the guy always attracted plenty of women. Rowdy women. Rance and Jayden were buddies, and had gotten into trouble together at a few bars on the rodeo circuit.

"We're each buying you a dance." Rance held up a fifty. "I'll get the first one." He pointed to a cute blonde, then rapped his knuckles on the pole. She nodded and jumped up on the table.

Dallas took a breath and prepared for a crazy night.

Two hours later, after Boone had accepted five lap dances, he stood and made a slashing motion. "That's all I can take, fellas. Anyone wanna go upstairs with me and see what the girls are doing?"

"Yeah." Dallas stood. He'd been thinking of Kira, wondering what she was up to. Was she a quiet watcher like he was? Tipping the dancers, but not buying himself lap dances? Or was she leading the zaniness, like Rance? Probably somewhere in the middle…he hoped.

Jayden and Rance both jumped up, Jayden slid out of the booth, Rance went over the top of the table. Somebody'd had plenty enough to drink. Maybe too much. Dallas had limited himself, sliding the shots they bought for him across the table. It just wasn't his idea of a good time, getting sloppy drunk.

The four of them walked up the steps. The music filling the stairwell changed from sexy and feminine in the female dancers' area to hard and thumping coming from where the men danced.

They stepped into a dark room with purple and red floodlights. Right inside the door, a couple stood, the woman held a drink in one hand and with the other, petted the chest of a man wearing only a Tarzan loincloth.

Dallas couldn't help the way his lip curled. He wouldn't be staying up here long, that was certain.

On an L-shaped stage, a man danced in thong underwear, smiling stupidly as a redhead slid folding money into his... Redhead? "Shit." He'd know that hair anywhere. Kira and the other five girls sat on chairs along the stage, their backs to the door where Dallas and the other cowboys stood. A fluffy white veil revealed which one was Gigi.

Boone leaned over. "I'm taking mine," he shouted. "We'll grab one of the Hummers." He looked at Dallas. "Make sure everyone gets in the other one okay."

Dallas nodded, already having planned to round them up and herd them back to the hotel.

Boone pointed a finger at Jayden, pinning him with a glare. "Make sure nothing happens to Stormie."

When Jayden lifted his hands and gave his brother an innocent look, Boone used his finger to poke Jayden in the chest. "Nothing. Got it?"

Jayden knocked Boone's hand aside. "Yeah, yeah. Just get your woman and get out of here. We'll be safe with old Dallas here in charge."

Boone stared at his brother, then shook his head, as if giving up.

Dallas took the insult and swallowed it. He couldn't help being the responsible person he was. Hell, if he ever let loose, his buddies would have him locked up and examined for extraterrestrial infiltration.

Boone smacked Dallas on the shoulder. "Thanks for an outstanding night." He looked at Dallas and Jayden. "You guys really pulled it together for me."

Dallas had done all the planning. Jayden had taken half the credit, but it didn't matter. It was Boone's last fling before he settled down. He just wanted his buddy to have a good time.

Boone strolled to where their women sat. He bent and whispered something to his fiancée, and she stood and threw her arms around him. Boone dipped her backward, real low, kissing her soundly.

The other girls stood and cheered, someone put a spotlight on the kissing couple, and the crowd joined in the hoots. The two of them parted, Gigi grabbed her little purse and turned to hug each of her friends. The front of her shirt was lit with multicolored lights announcing, "Bride to Be."

Rance laughed. "Bet Boone gets a shock trying to get her out of that contraption."

Dallas smiled and pulled out his camera,

hitting the video button to record Boone and Gigi.

Jayden nudged the other cowboy. "Hey, that's my future sister-in-law you're talking about."

"My apologies." Rance elbowed Jayden. "But wasn't it you who told me my sister was the hottest piece you'd seen in a month?"

Jayden had the smarts to dip his head. "All right. We're both pigs."

When Boone bent and swept Gigi up into his arms, a loud "Awww" went up from a hundred female voices. Still in the spotlight, they walked toward the door.

Dallas filmed the scene to be used as footage at their wedding reception.

Gigi gave the three of them a finger wave as Boone carried her past them and out the door.

"Cowboys!" a very loud female voice called as the spotlight landed on Rance, Jayden, and him.

"Oh shit." This was outside Dallas's comfort zone. He couldn't see much for the light in his eyes or he'd skedaddle.

The rest of the crowd took up the chant.

Jayden lifted his cowboy hat and swung it above his head, his grin downright naughty.

Rance set his fists on his hips and bulged out his chest, smiling and winking.

"Oh hell. Why not?" Dallas stuck his thumbs in his pockets, bracketing his package, and stood hipshot like Jayden had shown him. He forced a wide smile.

Over the din of the cheering women, he heard Kira's voice. "That's my cowboy!"

Dallas lifted a hand in a gunshot move toward

her general direction.

He heard her laughter ring across the room.

The music changed to a famous song about riding a cowboy instead of a horse. "C'mon boys, show us your stuff," the DJ called over the speakers.

In the seconds it took for Rance and Dallas to give each other the "let's get out of here" nods, Jayden had stepped forward. The spotlight followed him.

"There he goes." Rance leaned back against the doorjamb. "And he calls me crazy."

Dallas pulled out his phone and pressed the video record button. "You are crazy, bull rider. But that boy's one head injury short of being certifiable."

****

Kira watched as Jayden used Gigi's empty chair to step up on the stage.

A bouncer shouted for him to get down, but the DJ said, "Let's see what he's got for us, right, ladies?"

The crowd went wild.

"Unreal." Kira looked at Stormie.

Her cousin's eyes were wide and her smile a little shocked. "Oooh, look at him."

"That's what you want to get yourself mixed up with?" Kira gestured to Jayden as he strode along the stage just grinning at the women who held up dollar bills toward him.

"He's so cute." Stormie laid her hand over her heart.

"Oh no you don't." Kira pinched her cousin's arm. "Snap out of it. No rodeo cowboys, hear me?"

Stormie gave her the evil eye. "Like you and Dallas weren't banging around up in your suite this afternoon."

Kira had no response to that slice of truth.

Jayden finished his tour of the stage and called, "Stormie!"

She turned toward him as he ran and fell to his knees, sliding to a stop in front of her. "Wanna stick a dollar in my pants?"

Kira rolled her eyes. "Really?"

Stormie laughed like a teenager. "I can think of a few more interesting things I'd like to stick in there."

Kira grimaced. "Really?"

Jayden jumped down from the stage, took Stormie's hand, and tugged her with him toward the exit.

Kira made a few steps to follow, but Dallas stopped Jayden at the door. A lot of angry gestures flew between them, some finger pointing, then Dallas nodded, listened to whatever Stormie had to say, and let them go.

Grabbing her purse, Kira stomped to where Dallas stood next to another cowboy she'd seen outside the casino earlier. "Why did you let them go?"

He took her arms in his big hands. "They're okay. They just want to spend some time alone together. Jayden promised nothing would happen except some kissing."

"And you believe him because…" She tilted her head, waiting.

"Because Stormie promised to leave Jayden a virgin when she finished with him."

Kira broke out laughing.

Dallas grinned then laughed, too.

"God, I hope she does. He does." She waved her hands. "I hope both of them don't."

Dallas put his arm around her shoulders. "I'll call and check on them later." He turned her to face the other cowboy. "Kira, meet Rance. He rides bulls."

She held out her hand as the other three women in the bachelorette party joined them. She and Rance shook hands, and Kira introduced the cowboys to Gigi's and her friends from New York, Annie, Taylor, and Bree.

Taylor looked a little shocked behind her heavy glasses, but she was the quiet one of the group. This whole night had been a little over the top. Petite and mousy, she had barely said a word when they'd had dinner at Gigi's favorite restaurant overlooking the huge outdoor fountains on the strip.

When they'd stopped at two clubs and gone out onto the dance floor as a group, Taylor stayed on the periphery, never jumping into the middle of their dance circle.

Rance tugged Taylor's high ponytail. "You're kinda quiet, little missy. Everything okay?"

Taylor hugged her purse to her chest and nodded, her lips tightly pursed.

"C'mon." Dallas included all the women and Rance. "Let's go get the rest of those cowboys and take the Hummer somewhere we can dance."

Everyone else headed downstairs, leaving Dallas and Kira standing close together.

Kira tapped the big championship buckle he wore. "Do I get to polish your buckle, cowboy?"

"Sweetheart…" He kissed her temple. "You can polish anything of mine you like."

Kira licked her lips. When she got him alone… "I want to taste you, take you all the way into my mouth. All the way down my throat."

Dallas did his growl and his eyes narrowed. "Yeah?"

"Mm hm. And I want to swallow you, swallow your head and your cum and suck you dry, then lick you clean."

"Kira." He glanced around. "Let's get a cab and go—"

"Nope." She patted his belly. "Dancing first, then sexing."

"Sexing. Great." He took her hand and led her down the stairs. "But I'm warning you. We'll be dancin' mighty fast."

Two hours later, Dallas half-carried Kira into their suite. The woman could dance, but definitely lacked the ability to hold her liquor.

"…and then Taylor said, 'I don't approve of harming animals for profit', and Rance says, 'You don't know one thing about rodeo, city girl. So don't go making generalizations…' and that's when Taylor threw her drink in his face."

"Shit." Dallas hadn't witnessed the scene, but he'd seen the death stares Taylor and Rance gave each other in the Hummer on the way back to the hotel.

Kira tripped and dropped her purse. "Oops."

Picking her up in his arms, he carried her into the bedroom. Her suitcase and his duffle bag stood where they'd left them earlier when they grabbed them from their rooms before heading down to meet everyone in front of the casino.

"Turn off your phone, cowboy." Her words slurred slightly.

"Not gonna happen." Setting her down on the bed, he slid off her sandals. "Let me get your toothbrush."

"Why would I brush my teeth before I fill my mouth with your sweet cum?" Her smile wobbled and she blinked to keep her eyes open.

Dallas bit his cheek to keep from laughing. "You talk a sexy seduction, sweetheart, but you'd probably pass out halfway through."

She smacked him on the arm. "Not if you come quick enough."

He took a deep breath. He'd never taken advantage of an overserved woman before, and he wouldn't start tonight. "While that sounds very…appealing, let's just lie down for a little while. At least until the room stops spinning." Around her. He'd had a half dozen beers and a shot, but spread out over seven hours, he was sober as a statue.

"Huh." She flopped back onto the red satin bedspread. "Just for a minute."

He lay on his side next to her. His beautiful lady. He shook his head. His temporary lady. She had a big life planned in the big city, and he wouldn't waste his time chasing her, wanting more from her than a week together.

"What's this?" She pulled at the gold chain that had slid out of his breast pocket.

He put his hand over hers. "Nothing." He'd bought it for her, but couldn't find the guts to present it to her. It'd send a message he didn't mean to give, and it could only cause trouble.

She gave him sad puppy eyes. "Please?"

"Yeah, but it's just… It's not…" Fuck. "Here." He hauled out the long chain with another length of chain dangling a little gold heart locket from it.

Kira sat up and sucked in a breath. "You bought me a Valentine's present?"

He huffed out a breath. "It's not much. It doesn't mean anything."

She didn't hear. Sliding the chain over her neck, she frowned down at the heart hanging below her breasts. "Strange how long it is."

Here came the embarrassing part. "It's not for… Okay, I bought it at the strip club."

"Aw, where real men go to shop."

He chuckled and sat up. "It doesn't go here." He touched her neck. "It goes here." He put his palm on her waist.

Her brows drew together. "Oh yeah?" Taking off the chain, she unbuttoned her dress and pulled it off. Unfastening the clasp on the chain, she wrapped it around her waist and fastened it. The heart landed on her hip. She shook her hips and nearly lost her balance.

He knelt in front of her. "The heart goes here." He slid the chain around so the dangling heart on the chain lay against her mound.

"Oh." She bit her lip. "That's sexy."

He kissed her through the lacy blue panties she'd worn all day. The panties he wanted to rip off right now and slide his fingers, his tongue, then his hard cock into her soft, slick cunt. His mouth watered, wanting her, but he stood and pulled back the covers. "Sleep for a while. I'll get you some water and aspirin."

He walked out to the bar, pulled out a cold water, walked to the bedroom door, and found her asleep. He set the water on the nightstand, covered her with the quilt, and toed off his boots. He lay next to her, on top of the covers.

The last thing he saw before drifting off was her gorgeous face. His heart told him he could do this forever. His brain smashed that idea like an acorn under his boot heel.

He woke with light glowing in the room. The sun was up and shone off the buildings. He climbed out of bed and closed the drapes, went into the bathroom, and came out ready for a few more hours sleep.

Kira was gone. "Damn it." She'd slipped out on him. Probably heading down to the casino manager's office to claim the jackpot. All of it. "Fuck." He shouldn't have let himself trust her. He grabbed his boots and ran out of the bedroom.

Chapter Seven

"What's the hurry, cowboy?"

Dallas turned to find Kira, naked except for the chain and locket, coming out of the suite's other bathroom.

"Sweetheart." Relief flowed through him, followed by an explosion of lust.

"I never got what I wanted last night." She ran her hands from her hips to her breasts and tweaked her nipples. "Let me suck you, cowboy."

His hands went numb as desire pulled all his blood to one spot. His boots dropped to the floor. "Yeah, okay." Had dumber words ever been spoken?

"Remember at the strip club?" She ran a finger down the middle of her body to where the golden locket lay nestled in her short hairs. "Remember I said I wanted to taste you? Take your cum?"

He'd been thinking of nothing else all night. He nodded.

"I need you." She crooked her finger at him. "And I'm in charge tonight."

"It's morning." He bit back a smile.

"Whatever." She walked to the wall of windows and pressed her back against it. "Bring that big, oversized, shiny belt buckle over here and let me have some fun."

"Kira." Her ass pressed against the glass. They were on the top floor, but people may still be able to see her. Was this her kinky side coming out? He kinda liked it. "Are you sure you can handle such a big buckle?" He walked toward her.

"Dallas." She knelt and reached for him, grabbing his jeans pocket and pulling him to her. "I'm damn sure." In seconds she had his jeans down around his ankles and stroked his hard cock through his underwear.

"I'm not sure." He glanced out the window, wondering if people were looking. If anyone had a telescope. If…

She freed his cock and took the head into her hot, wet mouth.

Caution flew from his brain. Blasts of tiny spikes shot along his cock, into his balls, gathering at the base of his spine. He stomped down the urge to let go immediately. She was good.

Licking his slit, she sucked his head and worked her teeth gently against that spot on the bottom of his head where any touch drove him mad. Her heat nearly set him off.

Her fingers caressed his thighs as she sucked him in further, along the roof of her mouth and down to her throat.

"Kira, sweetheart."

She took him fully down her throat, the tightness around his head pulsing heat along his shaft.

Easing back, she kept the suction so tight he could imagine her taking the cum right out of his balls.

He ran his hand along her hair, impossibly soft against his rough palm. "Sweetheart. You're making me weak."

Looking up at him, she performed a dozen quick, deep strokes.

Quivers shot up his spine, rattling his brain, turning everything wobbly.

Using her fist, she found the spot behind his balls and massaged.

"Shit, shit, shit." The combination of her deep throat and her touch nearly made him shoot. "Stop."

She froze with his staff halfway in her mouth.

He pulled back, sliding out his cock. The pop of the suction releasing rattled heat through him. "I need to be inside your pussy." Reaching into the pocket of his jeans, he pulled out a condom packet then kicked away his pants.

She reached her arms up toward him, a sweet, sexy smile on her lips. "You want me?"

He slid his hands under her arms and lifted her. "Goddamnit, I want you bad."

Running her hands along his arms, she kissed him. "I can be bad."

"I know you can, sweetheart." A wild notion took him by surprise, and he went with it. Pressing her bare back against the window, he lifted her arms above her head. "But guess what? Sometimes a cowboy's gotta go bad, too." He tore open the packet with his teeth and rolled on the condom with one hand.

Her breath caught and she turned her head, looking out on the city. "Dallas. Yes. Take me here."

Releasing her wrists, he cupped her ass with one big hand and lifted her, resettling her against the glass. With his other hand, he lifted one of her legs, spreading her wide. Careful not to push her against the window, he slid his cock into her slick, tight pussy.

"Aw Kira." His spine quaked as flares shot upward, into his head, threatening to end the sensual agony of holding back his climax.

She wrapped her arms around his neck and kissed a sensitive spot he'd never realized he had, just under his ear, down to his collarbone.

The added sensory input clicked his brain closer to the edge of bliss.

Angling his hips, he rubbed the hair on his abdomen against her, tightening his muscles to brush against her clit with each pump of his cock. He knew he'd reached her nub when her kisses turned to bites, her body tensed, and her breathing became needy moans.

She moved her hips, taking more of him inside her, rubbing her clit harder against him, and sliding her diamond-hard nipples against his chest. "Yes, I'm coming. Now, Dallas."

He pistoned harder, driving into her, letting his body fracture as his shaft swelled with a last burst of blood, his balls pumped cum into her, and his head spun with his release, flashes of light colliding and shattering. Rolling waves of heat trickled down his spine and flared in his belly, pumping another load of cum through his cock.

Gradually his brain function returned, and his eyesight was restored. He caught her soft whispers against his neck.

"Dallas. You're amazing. Every time, it's better."

"Kira, girl, you're..." He had to stop speaking

before he blurted something that he'd regret. Like the word "love" or "forever" or "move in with me." Instead, he kissed her, pulling his staff out of her slick, warm slit and gently set her on her feet.

She wobbled, and he picked her up, carrying her to the couch. "Wait a second." From the bedroom closet, he grabbed a blanket and wrapped her in it. "Be right back."

After using the bathroom, he sat beside her on the couch and pulled her into his arms.

She snuggled in, closing her eyes. "Tell me about your parents."

He blinked back from the near doze he'd fallen into. "Okay." He didn't talk about them much, but this was Kira, and after what they'd shared already, it felt okay.

"Gigi told me they died, and that you live in an apartment in Reno, but that's all." She looked up at him, her eyes a soft shade of green. "Maybe I shouldn't have asked."

"No." He snuggled her head back against his chest. "It's fine. They died when I was nineteen. A...house fire."

She sucked in a breath and wrapped her arm around his waist, holding tight.

"I was already on the rodeo circuit. I had to fly home from Denver." The coroner hadn't let him see the bodies, but horrible pictures of what they must have looked like were never far from his thoughts. "They'd died in their sleep of smoke inhalation."

"That's a...small comfort." Her voice shook.

"It is." Kissing the top of her head, he inhaled her floral scent. "I had what was left of the house razed, the foundation dug out and filled in. I rent the land out to Boone's parents to farm."

"Is it close to their property?" She lifted her head and smiled. "Evidently, huh? Or else they couldn't farm it."

He ran his knuckles on her cheek. Damn, the way she made him feel; happy, relaxed, even when he spoke of the most depressing pieces of his life. "It adjoins theirs, and part of it runs along Boone's property, where we want to open the rodeo school."

"That's great. Are you going to use the land as part of the school?"

"Possibly, depending on how much room we need to pasture the livestock."

Her smile lit her face. "Isn't it exciting? You have the money to make that happen."

Nodding, he watched her for any hint of deception. "With my half of the jackpot, we can move forward a bit faster."

Her eyes shifted and she laid her head back onto his chest. "Maybe a lot faster."

What did she mean by that? Why wasn't he able to trust her? He laid his head on the back of the couch. God, he had problems. "Your turn. What's the story of your family?"

No answer. Her deep, even breaths told him she was asleep.

****

A persistent beeping woke Kira. She opened her eyes to the furry, warm chest of her cowboy.

He snored lightly.

The beeping was her phone about to die. She kissed Dallas's chest gently, covered him with the blanket, and slid away. They'd had a wild night and very little sleep. She planned to plug in her phone and crawl right back into his arms for more nap time.

Locating her purse under the entryway table, she pulled out her phone and brought it into the bedroom. She found her charger in her suitcase and plugged in the phone. "Five messages?"

How had she not heard them? "Oh yeah." She'd turned her phone to vibrate on the way up to the suite this morning with Dallas. Accessing voice mail, she heard the first message. Stormie, whispering, asking her to call her right away. Oh no, was something wrong?

The next message was her cousin again. "Jayden told me something, Kira. Call me. I'll keep my phone in my bra so I can hear it."

In her bra? Crazy Stormie. What could Jayden have told her that she needed to know so desperately. Her head swung toward the open bedroom door. Dallas. It had to be something about him.

The next two messages were Stormie waiting for a callback, but the fifth, sent at five in the morning, laid it all out. "Okay, I've got to tell you this, and I'm sorry to do it over the phone. Jayden said the only reason Dallas is with you right now is because he doesn't trust you to split the jackpot. He said that when you went back to the casino guy's office, Dallas figured you were working a double-cross."

A lump of fear plugged Kira's airway. Was that true?

"Jayden was a little drunk…okay, really drunk, when he told me, so I don't know if he was making it up or what. But it sounded like something you needed to know. Anyway, it was good to see you. The folks and I are heading back to OKC around nine this morning, so I probably won't get a chance to say goodbye."

Kira heard Jayden's voice in the background. He sounded a little drunk.

"Gotta go, cousin. Love ya!" Stormie had hung up.

Kira set down her phone, closed the bedroom door, then walked into the bathroom. Her face in the mirror looked pale and her eyes looked tired. Was she tired of fighting Dallas's distrust of life, of everyone? Of her, too? Maybe Stormie was wrong. Maybe Jayden was talking out of his ass. God knows the kid was full of bullshit. Dallas's behavior hadn't seemed devious.

But she needed to be sure. She'd test Dallas, give him one chance. She didn't want to give up on him based on her gut instinct plus a drunken cowboy's ramblings.

She laughed humorlessly as she started the shower. How pathetic. She was so attached to Dallas, she was willing to ignore her own instinct? As the water warmed, Kira called her attorney and made sure he was in Vegas, and would be at the eleven o'clock meeting.

An hour later, at ten o'clock, Kira leaned over the back of the couch looking at Dallas as he slept, sprawled along the length of it. So handsome, so innocent in his sleep. All she wanted to do was crawl in next to him and enjoy the little time they had remaining together. But she had to know the truth.

She hated to do this. Hated that she felt she had to test him to alleviate her own suspicions.

Dressed and packed, she wheeled her suitcase and banged it against the side table next to the couch.

He didn't wake.

She tried it again, this time with a little shout.

That did it. He hefted in a breath, gave a little cough, and sat up.

She walked toward the door, quietly, as if sneaking out.

"Hey." He jumped up, buck-naked. Pulling the blanket around his waist, he stumbled after her. "Where are you going?"

"I'm just…" She made her voice sound casual, went for an innocent facial expression. "I was going to say goodbye to Stormie."

His brows drew together. "With your suitcase?"

She shrugged. "We have to check out soon, don't we? I thought I'd leave my bag at the valet desk and pick it up later when I have to head to the airport."

He stepped forward and took her wrist—the one holding the suitcase—in his hand.

"Stay. I'll call for a late checkout."

She let go of the bag and it stood itself upright. "Okay. Sure. I'll just go find Stormie."

He didn't release her. "Wait until after I shower. We'll go together."

She tugged her wrist out of his grip. "Dallas. You're acting like you don't trust me."

His jaw tightened and his lips thinned. "Is there a reason I shouldn't trust you?"

"No."

After staring into her eyes for a few seconds,

he looked away. "Will you just wait for me? I'll hurry."

Her heart dropped like a rock off a cliff. He didn't trust her. Not only did he not trust her, but he didn't have the emotional depth to confront her with his suspicions. She needed time to consider this. Needed to figure out what to do next.

"Of course I'll wait." She set down her purse. "Take your time showering. I'll call and see where Stormie is." Halfway to Oklahoma by now, but Dallas didn't have to know that.

He pushed her suitcase aside.

She walked to the windows and dialed Stormie's number.

A few minutes later, the shower started in the bathroom.

"Hi Kira."

Stormie sounded perky, as usual.

"Hi. Where are you?"

As Kira turned to have a seat, she spotted Dallas watching her from the bedroom. Damn. He really didn't trust her. The knowledge was like a bullet to the gut.

"We're still crossing Arizona. We'll probably spend the night in Albuquerque." Strange sounds came through the phone. "Kira…" Her voice was soft. "About what Jayden said, it could have been just the beer talking."

"I'm not worried, Stormie. I'll figure it out on my own." She leaned over and saw Dallas in the shower. "How did it go with you and Jayden?"

Stormie let out a small squeal. "You won't believe it." She said something to someone in the car. "I'll call you later and we can talk."

"Okay. Your parents are listening, right?"

"Oh yes, always." She sounded disgusted. "Talk to you later!"

"I can't wait." She hung up. What could have happened to make her cousin so excited? She laughed. What *didn't* make Stormie excited?

Dallas stepped out of the shower, grabbed a towel and walked to the bedroom door.

Checking to see if she was still there? Probably.

"Where's Stormie?"

"She's on her way home. So we have time to grab something to eat before we meet the manager."

"Time?" He ruffled a towel over his hair, his body naked and gorgeous. "I thought we could be there any time today?"

She swallowed. Caught in a lie. "I called and arranged our meeting with him at eleven." She shrugged. "I'm kind of an organizational freak."

With a nod, he went back into the bedroom and dressed.

Their meal was delicious. He had the Cowpoke's Breakfast, a platter full of fattening delights. She chose a chef's salad with salmon. They both picked at each other's plates. As if everything was just fine. As if he trusted her, and she didn't know he didn't.

When they walked into the casino manager's office, the junior partner of her family's attorney's office stood.

"Hi Barret. Thanks for coming." She shook his hand.

"Who's this?" Dallas's face turned red under

his tan.

"Dallas Burns, this is my attorney, Barret Weis. Barret, this is the man with whom I won the jackpot."

Barret held out his hand.

Dallas glared at Kira. "Why is he here?"

Chapter Eight

"Uh…" Barret Weis, Kira's family attorney, glanced at the three others in the casino manager's office then dropped his hand. He looked directly at Dallas as he answered the cowboy's question. "Ms. Morrow called our office yesterday and asked me to handle the situation here at the casino for her."

The casino manager sat. "It's all settled, Ms. Morrow." He set a stack of papers on the desk. "You just need to sign here." He pointed with a pen.

Dallas growled. "You're taking the entire jackpot."

Barret gave a small laugh. "She's *giving* the entire jackpot. To you."

Dallas jerked as if hit by a lightning bolt. "What was that again?"

The casino manger stood, probably since no one else had taken a seat. "We have regulations about releasing funds only to the rightful winner, but we have, in the past, come to legal agreements, providing all necessary tax burden questions are addressed, to provide alternative—"

"Hang on." Dallas put up his hand toward the manger, but looked directly at Kira. "You're saying you want to give me all the money."

"That's what I'm saying." She picked up the pen and signed on the line. "There. It's all yours."

The manager sat, and so did her attorney.

"Now, Mr. Burns." The manager set another stack of papers closer to Dallas. "If you would, please."

Dallas's gaze didn't veer from hers. "Why? Why don't you want the money?" His face told her he still didn't trust her. He was expecting a trick.

Barret cleared his throat. "Kira is from one of the twenty richest families in New York."

She watched Dallas's face turn from red to white.

"So, one day, you'll inherit? You'll be rich?"

She opened her mouth, searching for the right words.

"Kira has already inherited millions of—" Barret blurted.

"Please." She turned to her attorney. "Barret, thank you." She glanced at the manager's nametag. "Mr. Truman?"

"Please, call me Ray."

"Ray. Is there somewhere that Mr. Burns and I can talk?"

The manager stood. "You're welcome to my office for as long as you like." He stepped toward the door. "Mr. Weis, would you care for a cup of coffee?"

Barret looked at Kira. She nodded. He handed her a large brown envelope. "Here's that other matter you'd asked me to look into." He frowned at Dallas then glanced back at her. "We had success."

Relief flowed through her. At least one thing had gone right.

The moment the door closed, Dallas crossed his arms, a look of complete irritation on his face.

"Another background check on me, I assume."

"No." Asshole. She bit back the anger. She'd probably be just as angry if she were in his shoes. Boots. "Oh hell." She flopped down in a chair. "Let me explain."

Instead of sitting next to her, he leaned back against the desk. Always on guard. Always cautious.

"Dallas, why don't you trust me?" She didn't mean to jump right in, but now that she was hip deep… "I mean, I know why. Your history. Your very recent history, especially." She glanced up into his suspicious eyes. "But why me in particular. What did I do to make you distrust me?"

"At the roulette table, you were going on about having the money direct deposited. You warned me that I had to play by your rules or I wouldn't get a penny." He braced his hands on the desk on each side of his thighs and leaned over her. "Then after our meeting here yesterday, you ran back in for God knows what." He sat back. "Some lie about your gold pen." He flung a hand toward her purse. "Which is probably real gold, too."

The accusation in his voice nearly made her heart crumble.

"I told you I would give you half. You couldn't believe me?"

"I did." His voice rolled low and fierce. "Until you went back into the manager's office."

She sat back and crossed her arms, letting her temper rise a bit. "You want the truth?"

"Please." The word cracked like a whip.

"At first, I wanted to push you. To see if you'd snap, become…violent."

"Fuck." He said it through clenched teeth.

"Then I realized that the court found you not guilty because you were innocent." She let the feeling of that pivotal moment wash through her like a calming stream. "Then…" This was going to be the difficult part. Opening her heart to him. "I didn't tell you about giving you the entire jackpot because I wanted to keep you close." A wave of emotion threatened tears. "I wanted to see if you were as amazing as I remembered you from December."

"Huh." He didn't look or sound quite as angry.

She wouldn't reveal everything, though. She'd keep the secret that she did find him as amazing— more amazing—than she'd thought him back then. "I wanted to see where this connection between us led. I wanted you in bed, Dallas. And I wanted to see the surprise on your face when I told you I was giving you the whole jackpot." She looked at his wary expression and her eyes misted. That whole plan sure went to hell.

"Kira."

His cold tone told her everything. She stood and stared at a spot over his shoulder. "I'm sorry I didn't mention I was filthy rich. It just didn't come up, and it's not something I wear on a LED lighted T-shirt for the world to see."

She held the brown envelope in two hands. She wanted to surprise him with its contents, too, but her surprises today had turned to disasters.

"I'm just having a hard time taking all this in." He turned his back to her and stared at the video monitor of the casino. "Let's take some time to sort this out. Slow things down." He was protecting his heart.

She didn't blame him, but she'd been too stupid to do the same for her own heart. "That's okay, Dallas." She made her voice as chipper as Stormie's. "It's run its course, you and me. We're polar opposites, and nothing we do will ever change that."

He watched her from over his shoulder.

Kira walked to the door. "I'll be in the suite until I have to leave for the airport." She tried a smile but it didn't work. "I'll have a bellman pick up your bag, and you can get it from the valet desk."

When he didn't speak, she lifted a hand in farewell and walked out, leaving the door open. She gestured for Ray and Barret to head back into the office. "Thank you both." She noted their uncertain faces, but didn't have the energy to reassure them. "I'll be here for three more hours if you need to call me for anything." She kept walking.

Dallas didn't say another word. Didn't call to her to stop, didn't charge after her and pick her up in his arms to proclaim his apology.

"So long, cowboy," she whispered.

****

Dallas felt like he was underwater. Had Kira just walked away from him? Had he fucking just let her go? He wanted to move, wanted to haul ass after her, but years of playing it safe—on everything but a bucking bronc's back—kept his boots glued to the floor.

The manager and attorney came back in, closed the door, and quietly sat in their seats, as if a loud noise or quick movement would trigger an explosion in Dallas.

He forced his muscles to relax and sat, signed where he was supposed to, accepted a check for nearly two hundred thousand dollars as if it were a grocery receipt, and stood to leave.

Barret held out a card. "Call me if you'd like some help with tax shelters on that money. I understand you're investing in a business. We can work out the best plan for your bottom line."

"Kira told you about the business?" He didn't know how to react to that news.

"Yes, she did." The attorney picked up his briefcase. "I hope you don't mind, but I did some research on similar businesses, and I have some ideas for you and your partners." He leaned closer. "All at well discounted rates, since you're a new client, and our company prides itself in assisting startups like yours."

"I…" He couldn't believe the luck he was having. "Sure. We'll be in touch." He held out his hand.

Barret shook it. His grip was firm. "And secretly…" He lifted his brows. "I've always wanted to ride a bull."

The casino manager laughed. "Haven't we all." He stood and shook both men's hands. "But some of us have gotten past the age of actually doing it." He opened the door and escorted them down the hallway to the casino. "Best of luck to you, Mr. Burns. And Mr. Weis, don't break any bones at that rodeo school."

Dallas and the attorney said goodbye and Dallas went straight to the Roundup Bar and ordered a beer in a longneck bottle.

One of only five people in the bar, he could

have sat anywhere, but he took a stool facing the booth where he and Kira and the gang had celebrated their jackpot win. Was it just yesterday? He burped but the hollow feeling under his heart didn't go away. Or was it inside his heart?

"Kira." Funny, he'd always figured that when he remembered her, it would be the times they'd had sex. Her full lips around his cock, her sweet pussy around his tongue, her breasts as he sucked them to perfect peaks.

Nope. It was her teasing smiles, the look she had when she wasn't about to let him get away with his bullshit, her soft, consoling glances when he'd talked about his past.

He slammed his bottle on the bar.

The cute, exotic-looking bartender brought him another.

"Sorry." He drank the last ounces and set down the empty. "Rough morning."

"This one's on me, then." She winked and walked away.

This was his chance to move on. He had a big check in his pocket, he could talk Jayden into staying another night and driving home to Reno tomorrow, and the way the bartender was bending over to check the stock in the cabinet, he could have a warm, willing, no-strings sex partner tonight.

He looked away from her ass. He was an ass. He could have Kira in his bed tonight. He stood. He could have Kira in his arms right now. He could get things back the way they were this morning. She hadn't told him to stay away, threatened a restraining order, or a knee to the groin if she ever saw him again.

All he had to do was apologize. Make things right, deal with what happened in the casino office, and he could have her back. Have her today, have her again next weekend in New York. Get his fill of her and say goodbye after the wedding.

As he pulled out his wallet, something inside him turned cold at the plan. Would it be enough? "It'd have to be enough."

"What was that, cowboy?" The bartender crossed her arms under her bountiful breasts.

"Thanks, ma'am." He set down a nice sized bill and touched the brim of his hat. "Much obliged."

She winked. "Come back any time. I'm off at six."

He nodded and turned. Hopefully by six, he and Kira would be tucked in bed in their suite enjoying supper in bed, with some chocolate and whipped cream waiting to be spread on heated body parts as dessert.

A few minutes later, he knocked and slid the keycard in the door of the Wrangler Suite.

Kira walked out of the bedroom, her eyes red, her cheeks wet. "Did you forget something?" She turned toward the bedroom. "I thought I packed every—"

"Kira. Sweetheart. I'm not here for anything but you."

She turned toward him so fast, she nearly toppled before catching herself on the doorjamb. "What?"

"I was wrong. I was an idiot. I am a fool, and I want you." He took off his hat and held it in both hands in front of him. He had to get this right the first time, had to convey his sincerity and his humility every way he could.

She narrowed her eyes. "What does this mean?" She seemed cold, as if a wall had dropped around her.

"I was wrong to not trust you, but please, see this from my perspective. I've been burned in the past. Badly. In the casino office, I found out about all the things you'd held back from me. You're rich, you're giving me the whole jackpot, you got your attorney working on it." Shit, he sounded like a whiny three year old.

Kira laced her fingers together in front of her. "I'm sorry. But I don't—"

"No, don't tell me to go." He set down his hat and walked toward her. "I'm not as sharp as you. It takes me a while to process things. To get things settled through my thick skull and into my brain." He took her hands, kissing each one softly. "I just now realized what I had with you. What I turned my back on."

She blinked rapidly. "What are you asking?"

"Let's start again. We have today." He touched her chin. "Maybe you can stay another night?"

"And then?"

He heard the uncertainty in her voice. "And then we have next weekend in New York." He offered a small smile. "It'll be fun. I'll try to resist keeping you in bed the whole 48 hours and you can show me the town." That sounded easy. No drama, no commitments.

She breathed heavily, as if fighting back tears.

"And then?"

"Do we have to decide right now? Can't we take it one day, one weekend, at a time?"

Kira closed her eyes and twin tears rolled down her cheeks. "I see." She looked up at him. "Damn you, Dallas Burns, I have no way to resist you."

His heart did a quickstep. "Sweetheart. Let me make it up to you." He moved closer and brushed his lips against hers. "Let me take the hurt away for both of us."

"Yes. Make love to me." The sorrow in her eyes nearly broke him.

He wiped away the tracks of her tears with his thumbs. "It'll be okay. You'll see." Did he really believe that? Had he convinced her, or himself, that half a promise was enough?

Chapter Nine

Casual. No strings. That's what her cowboy wanted. Kira reached up and unbuttoned his shirt. Fine. That's what he would get. One last time, she'd let herself be Dallas's woman. Let the escape of his powerful lovemaking take away the hurt for a little while.

Within seconds, they were both naked and Kira held the condom packet Dallas had pulled from his pocket. She walked backward toward the couch, forcing a seductive look to replace the dejected one that mirrored her inner thoughts.

She pointed to the couch. "Lay down, cowboy. I wanna ride."

"Aw sweetheart." Dallas took a running leap and landed on his back on the couch with a bounce and a grin. His big, hard cock slammed against his belly and rebounded, pointing to the suite's ceiling.

Despite Kira's inner turmoil, she smiled.

He patted his thighs. "Mount up, cowgirl."

She straddled his legs and rolled the condom on his beautiful, hot penis. Moving over him, she eased his head into her slit.

"Whoa. What's the hurry?" He grabbed her hips to stop her.

The faster she lost herself in passion, the quicker her heartbreak would stop hurting. For a while. Taking his hands, she placed them on her breasts. "I can't wait, big guy."

He worked her nipples gently.

She dropped her torso onto him, impaling herself. The slight pain she felt in her core was preferable to the vast one occupying her chest.

His fingers tugged at her nipples and groans of pleasure rumbled from his mouth.

She worked her thighs, riding fast and furiously, concentrating on the screaming muscles in her legs, the fullness inside her opening, and the building orgasm that barely overrode her sorrow.

Leaning down, she looked into Dallas's black eyes, loving the soul-deep intensity of them, memorizing it. She grasped his nipples and tugged them.

"I like that," he breathed.

The angle made it easier for her to speed up, to lose herself deeper in the motion and the sensation.

"Sweetheart. Gonna come." It rolled from him on a groan.

A whir of tingles raced up her spine and jingled at her brain. A weak orgasm, but bittersweet and unforgettable as her last with the man she…loved. She gasped as emotion broke free and flooded her eyes with moisture.

She'd said it, admitted it. She loved him. Nothing in her life compared to the sweetness and the pain of knowing she loved. And lost.

She held in the sobs as Dallas tensed and pumped upward, coming inside her, shouting, "Kira."

With her next breath, the damn broke. She dropped her head as a sob wracked her body and tears flowed, dripping onto his chest. She sucked in another breath and silently wept out her frustration and sorrow.

He froze. "Sweetheart." He pushed her hair back from her face. "Aw God, Kira. Are you hurt?"

"N…no."

"Are you just really happy we're back together?"

"No, you asshole." The anger helped, pulling her back from the edge of hysterics.

He lifted her off him and settled her on his chest, but she shoved free and stood, stumbling before she got her footing.

"I can't be with someone…" She puffed in uneven breaths. "Who can't trust anyone. Can't trust me." She swiped her hands across her cheeks to wipe away the tears. They would be the last ones she cried for him.

He slid onto his side and patted the couch in front of him. "Come here and let me hold you, sweetheart. We can talk about this. All night if you want."

"No more talking. No more touching. No sex, no cuddling. This is the end." It tore her apart to say it, but at the same time, she felt stronger, empowered.

"I feel like shit." He covered his eyes with his forearm. "I came at this all wrong, didn't I."

"No, you went right where your ultra careful brain directed. But I'm not going along for the ride. You want casual sex, and I…" Shit, what did she want? "I guess I need more."

He looked at her. "I'm not ready to promise…more."

"Will you ever be?" Her body shook with the

letdown after sex, after her crying jag.

Dallas was silent.

That spoke louder than a gunshot. "I'm sorry. I used you just now. I wanted one last time, one chance to ease the pain." She was a horrible person. "I let you believe we'd be doing this…" She gestured between their naked bodies. "Until after the wedding, but I shouldn't have." When she sighed, it drained all her strength. "I made you believe I wanted to be your plaything."

"Plaything." He said it with so little passion, it sounded dry and nasty.

"I'll see you at the wedding, but I don't want to be with you then, like this. My heart can't take it. I'm a weak woman for such a loudmouthed redhead."

He sat up. "Where is this all coming from?"

"I've thought it through. Since I'll probably be seeing you when I visit Gigi in Reno, ending this now, spending next weekend as if we were just acquaintances, will help me move on."

He started to stand.

"No, stay there for a few minutes." She was a coward, but if he stood and held out his arms, she might just fold into them and accept his offer of a temporary relationship. She picked up her clothes from the floor, walked into the bedroom, hauling her suitcase with her, and shut the door, locking it behind her.

He knocked. "Kira. Let me in."

She ran into the bathroom and turned on the shower to flood out his voice. After rinsing off, she turned on the clock radio loud, drowning out any knocking or cajoling he might be doing. When she was dressed, she silenced the radio and picked up the brown envelope Barret had given her. She could give it to him now, but it might seem like a desperate attempt to buy his love. She'd hang on to it, give it to Dallas next weekend if the PI didn't have the buckle in hand by then. She shoved it in her big travel purse and wheeled her suitcase out of the bedroom.

He stood at the window fully dressed, heartbreakingly handsome

He walked quickly to her and reached out, taking her arms in his hands. "You don't have to leave for the airport yet. Sit down. Let's work this out."

As his touch on her arms warmed her cool body, his low, rugged voice pierced the place in her heart she was trying to numb. It wasn't what she wanted for her life, though. A fast, clean break right now was better than hanging on to him, hoping he'd change his mind and give her more of himself.

She stepped back, sliding out of his grip. "Happy Valentine's Day." She forced a smile. "See you next weekend."

It took all her strength to haul her suitcase toward the door, away from the man she wanted to be with so badly, it caused physical pain.

Of course, he said nothing, did nothing, as she opened the door and walked away.

****

Dallas watched Kira leave him. This was his last chance to call her back.

The door quietly closed. He was alone.

The silence buzzed around him like a swarm of locusts. He touched his back pocket where the casino's check sat in his wallet. Would it make his life complete? Were money and possessions the only things in his life that he trusted?

Kira had said he couldn't trust. He'd tried. He'd gone halfway, offered her today, tonight, next weekend. She wasn't a halfway woman, though. She was all or nothing, and he was still licking his wounds from the last woman he'd gone all-in for.

He walked to the bar and chose a beer from the fridge, then set it back inside and grabbed a bottle of water. He needed every brain cell to work through this one.

"Okay, feelings. Get in touch with my feelings." He sat in an armchair and stared at the mustang mural. What the hell was he feeling? Anger at himself for not being able to keep Kira here with him. Anger with her for cutting him off cold turkey. Hell, anger wasn't what he needed now.

He'd shut himself off from so many emotions that trying to dredge them up felt like hauling a rusty chain out of a dark pit. He looked at the refrigerator. Maybe he did need a beer.

A knock sounded at the door.

He jumped up. "Kira?" He rushed to the door and yanked it open.

Gigi and Boone look like they'd just rolled out of bed.

A worry line creased her forehead. "Kira just called and said she was on her way to the airport. What's going on?"

"I don't know." He stood back, gesturing them inside.

"Let me guess." Boone ushered Gigi into the suite ahead of him. "You fucked up."

Dallas closed the door. "Guess I did."

Admitting it to two people he admired burned like fire in his gut.

Gigi sat on the couch, patting the spot next to her for Dallas. "What happened? Weren't things going well?"

Dallas sat down beside her. "I thought they were, but it's confusing. I can't get my head around it."

Boone grabbed three beers from the bar, handed one to each of them, and sat on the other side of Gigi. "My very smart fiancée should be able to clear this up for you."

Gigi smiled at Boone then turned to face Dallas. "Tell us everything that happened."

He started with Kira's strange behavior in the back hallway of the casino the day before, told them about Jayden's suggestion to stick close to her in case she was trying to pull a quick one.

"And you listened to Jayden?" Gigi frowned.

"Afraid so." Dallas talked about Kira acting suspicious, and trying to leave the suite that morning, alone and with her suitcase, and how he'd kept her in the suite, kept an eye on her.

"Knowing Kira, I'd guess she was testing you." Gigi looked concerned.

Dallas set down the untasted beer. Gigi's guess seemed accurate. "And I failed the test." He looked at Gigi. "But do you blame me? What else was I supposed to do?"

"Talk to her." Gigi set down her beer, too. "Explain your concerns. Get a feel for what she's feeling."

Dallas stood and walked to the wall of

windows. "Feelings. Hell, I don't think I have them anymore." His heart felt heavy knowing he'd messed up so badly. Was that a feeling?

"Okay." Boone said. "So you went to the casino office and you each got your split."

Dallas spun around. "That's the thing. She didn't take half. She gave me all of it."

"What?" Boone's voice went up an octave.

"She's rich."

"She is?" Boone looked at Gigi. "You knew that, didn't you."

Gigi grimaced. "I knew her parents were rich, but she's pretty independent. I figured she'd take half the jackpot to pay off her school loans and—"

"No, she's got millions. She inherited it." Dallas watched for Gigi's reaction.

She sat forward, her eyes wide. "Really? She never said."

Boone scratched his cheek. "How did she work around the casino's regulations to give you the money?"

Pacing in front of the glass wall, Dallas told them about the attorney, and the words Kira had quietly spoken when they were alone. Words that had hit him like bricks. He explained that he'd given her some time, then come back to the suite and apologized. He'd thought things were back to normal, then she'd walked out. Again.

"Aw hell, buddy." Boone gestured to Dallas's beer. "Take a pull. You need a little numbing."

Dallas flopped into the armchair. "Sure do." His chest hurt, his head throbbed, and a feeling of panic built with each passing minute. "Problem is, when she walked away, she gave me what I asked for—a quick, clean end. Now I'm not sure that's what I want."

Gigi clasped her hands in front of her. "Tell me what you like about Kira."

"She's smart, beautiful, sexy, funny. She makes me happy." Her smiling face popped into his mind. "She doesn't let me get away with any of my BS."

"And you got plenty of that, buddy." Boone grinned.

Gigi turned to him and gave him a stern glance. The bull rider actually looked apologetic.

Was this what love was all about? Changing your bad habits just enough to make someone else happy?

Gigi caught Dallas's attention again. "That's good. What's one thing she does that makes you happy?"

"Well, she wanted to surprise me by giving me the entire jackpot." The disappointment on her face when he'd ruined it still haunted him.

"She's very generous. With her time and her…um…money." Gigi smiled. "I guess I know why, now. But what else about her?"

"She's adventurous." When he'd made love to her up against the wall of windows, his first instinct was to be more cautious, haul her into the bedroom, but he knew stepping out of his comfort zone would make her happy, so he'd done it, and had loved every second of it.

"She gets her own way, and makes me think it was my idea." When she wanted to go dancing, he was okay with it because dancing made her happy.

When she wanted to hear the story of his arrest, he told her, because she wanted to hear it, and he wanted to please her.

Boone cleared his throat. "That'd be every woman's trick."

Gigi smacked his leg. "Boone, you're not really helping here."

He held up his hands. "Okay, okay. I'll let the expert do her work." The cowboy stood and went to the bar for another beer.

"Dallas, what do you feel for her?" Gigi tucked her legs under her on the couch.

"Feelings aren't my thing." He felt his jaw tighten.

"Don't say them out loud, just see if you can experience them."

He heaved a sigh. When he'd gone into the gift shop at the strip club looking for something heart-shaped, and the only non-triple-x rated item was the hip chain. What had he been feeling then?

He thought about the picture Boone had sent him. The six of them and their giant liquor glasses. Dallas had ignored everyone but Kira. Her face, hopeful, sexy, excited. His lips had curled up as he'd stared into her beautiful eyes.

He liked her, wanted to make her happy, wanted to see her smile. Her smile made him happy.

"Happy." Something warm radiated around his heart. He'd never been happy with a woman. Even his relationship with Layna had been just a physical connection, something he'd grasped at, hoping an emotional tie would follow. It never did with Layna, but with Kira?

A bubble of something crept up his throat and

burst out of him as laughter. Was he going crazy?

"What's happening over there?" Boone leaned on the bar, watching him.

"I think Dallas has found what he's been looking for." Gigi's voice was soft.

Dallas glanced between her and Boone. "Does falling for someone and going nuts feel exactly the same?"

"Exactly the same." Boone said.

Gigi raised an eyebrow. "A girl *has* to be crazy to fall for a rodeo cowboy."

Is this what Kira was feeling for him? Is this why she wanted more from him? She wanted to take things a step further, find out how much better this feeling could get.

He took a breath and prepared to ask himself "the question." Did he love Kira? Excitement raced around his heart, sending it pattering wildly. The Valentine's Day mushy stuff had hit him. Hard. But was it love?

"He's gone silent again." Boone strode toward them. "This could be bad."

"Give him time. He's realizing just how amazing Kira is. How letting her in could be the best thing he's ever done in his life."

"Kira is a hell of a woman." Boone leaned on the back of the couch behind Gigi. "I've gotten to know her over the last few months. She and Dallas would be good for each other."

Gigi looked up at her fiancé. "They would. It's not so much that opposites attract, as it is both of them looking for something that the other can give them."

They weren't very damn subtle, but he'd play along. "Like what?"

She nodded at Boone.

The bull rider smiled at Gigi, and Dallas's chest clutched at the emotion in his gaze and the intensity in the look Gigi returned. He wanted that for himself. With Kira?

Boone pierced Dallas with a hard stare. "You've been alone since you were nineteen. When you turned twenty-eight last year, something made you want to settle down, and you did, but with the wrong woman. Now you're afraid to admit Kira might be the right woman because you nearly got destroyed once."

His friend was right. And more perceptive than Dallas had given him credit for. He was tired of being alone.

"Buddy." Boone set his hand on Gigi's shoulder but stared at Dallas. "Your instinct to find someone was right. Don't let what happened with Layna make you lose your chance with Kira."

Dallas's cautious side still warned him not to let the connection between him and Kira get too deep. It told him that jumping into another relationship this quickly was foolish. But his heart told him something different. Nearing the end of his rodeo career, he wanted to be part of a family. Make a family of his own. He could see him and Kira building a house on his property in Reno. Building a life and a family. Could she be happy on a ranch in Nevada?

"What could Kira need from an old broken-down bronc rider?" She was a millionaire. She could do anything, date anyone she wanted.

"Dallas, she doesn't know what she wants to

do with her life." Gigi laid her hand over Boone's on her shoulder. "Her family is in accounting. And while she did what was expected of her and got her degree in finance, she's not excited to work in her family's business."

"She never mentioned that." Dallas went back over the conversations he and Kira had. "She didn't mention anything about what she wants to do with her degree."

"Did you ask her?" Gigi's eyebrows lifted.

They'd talked about his parents, but never hers. "I guess I didn't." Why hadn't he asked again, after that first time when she'd fallen asleep? Why didn't he ask her about her life in New York? Had he been afraid of getting to know her better? Afraid it would lead to him getting too close to her?

"I hope Kira will forgive me for betraying her confidence when I say this." Gigi glanced at Boone before continuing. "After you and Kira met in December, she asked about you."

"A lot," Boone added. "She'd tune in to conversations whenever your name was mentioned." He chuckled. "Hell, if *I* noticed her interest in you, it had to be pretty damn obvious."

This was a lot for Dallas to take in. Kira wasn't happy in New York. She was interested in him, and she'd come right out and admitted she wanted to try a relationship with him. That thought alone made him want to run after her and drag her back to Reno with him. For good.

No, no running and no dragging. He had to figure this out. "I'll think about it, and when I'm in New York next week—"

"Dallas, don't be an idiot." Boone's voice echoed loudly in the room. "Do something now or she'll be gone forever."

Dallas looked at Gigi. She nodded. "I know Kira. If you wait, it'll be too late."

He stood and walked to the glass wall, looking out at the city. He could play it safe and do nothing, hope that if he decided to go for it next weekend, Kira would fall into his arms. That'd be the safest way. Then, if he decided this week that he didn't want her…

Fuck. Didn't want her? His breath stalled at the idea of not having her in his life. He wanted her so damn bad, his hands fisted and his heart thumped, ready for action.

He grabbed his phone from his pocket and pressed Contacts. K. Kira. He could call her, but she'd just send him straight to voice mail, and maybe block his number.

Spinning around, he looked at Gigi. "I don't know how, but I'm going after her. Right now."

Gigi squealed. "Thank God. Boone said you'd go for the grand gesture once you realized you loved her." She pulled her phone from her pocket.

He loved her. It didn't hurt to think it. It did generate a burst of fear, but he could live with that. It was Kira he couldn't live without. How could he get to her? She would be at the airport and probably through security already. With his head spinning from the word "love" banging around in it, he couldn't think. "What do I do?"

Dialing her phone, Gigi smiled. "Boone and I figured it out on the way to your suite." She held the phone to her ear. "Leave this one to me."

****

Kira sat in a wide vinyl chair at the gate where her flight would take her home to New York. When she'd walked through security three hours ago, her tension eased. Dallas couldn't get to her here.

She'd turned off her phone and wandered through the airport for an hour then went to the deserted gate and sat at a window seat watching airplanes arrive. Was it just two days ago she'd flown in? Full of excitement and expectation knowing she'd see Dallas again? It felt like a week. When they'd made love, it had been the most amazing experience of her life. She let out a breath. She'd miss it. She'd miss him.

Saying goodbye to him had been one of the— no—the hardest thing she'd ever done. In less than twenty-four hours, he'd slammed into her heart like a rank bull, and left his mark. Permanently.

How difficult would it be to see him next weekend? To not touch him, not kiss him, or stare into his incredible eyes?

Someone jostled her as they sat next to her. She'd been too spacey the last couple of hours to notice the area filling with travelers.

"We will now begin boarding flight 4214 to New York LaGuardia…"

Boarding already? Kira jumped up and looked for the girls. Gigi, Annie, and Bree should be here by now. Taylor was staying, renting a car and driving to San Francisco to visit her grandparents.

She spotted Annie and Bree standing by the boarding gate. Hauling her suitcase, she picked her way through the crowd. "Hi. Did you just get here?"

Both girls looked exhausted. Annie nodded. "We've been trying to call you."

"Sorry. I forgot to turn my phone back on." She looked around the area. "Where's Gigi?"

Bree's forehead wrinkled. "We thought she was coming with you. We haven't been able to get her on the phone, either."

A bubble of panic threatened, then she remembered who Gigi was with. "She's probably coming to the airport with Boone. He's flying up to Reno today."

The girls nodded. Bree yawned. "I'm going to have a cosmo and crash."

"We will now begin boarding first class…"

They moved into the line and in minutes were settled in their seats. Kira had the window seat in the last row of first class, and Bree and Annie were across the aisle from her. Gigi would be sitting next to Kira, whenever she decided to show up.

As promised, both Annie and Bree had ordered cosmos, slurped them down, and now rested under blankets, with pillows beneath their heads.

As people filed onto the airplane, Kira watched for Gigi. She turned on her phone. No call from Dallas. Had she expected one? Stupid cowboy. She deleted the four voicemails from Annie, then called Gigi. It went right to voicemail. Maybe she was in line to board the plane, and had turned it off.

Twenty minutes later, the last passenger had boarded, and no Gigi.

The flight attendant took a call, hung up the phone, and announced to first class, "We're waiting for one more passenger. It'll be just a few minutes."

Kira took her first real breath in a half hour.

That had to be Gigi.

Five minutes later, from near the cockpit door, the flight attendant said, "Welcome. You're in the last first class seat on your right."

Kira looked up but didn't see who the woman was talking to. It had to be Gigi. Thank God.

The voice that thanked the attendant wasn't Gigi's. Wasn't even female. It was low and growly.

Dallas walked down the aisle toward her. His black cowboy hat sat low on his head, and he wore a dark red cotton button down shirt tucked into his sexy jeans.

Her heart stopped for a couple seconds then restarted at an amazing rate. What was going on? Had something happened to Gigi? No, he was smiling at her.

The flight attendant found a spot for his duffle bag and inquired about stowing his hat, to which he thanked her but declined. The cowboy plopped into the seat next to her, and set a black shopping bag on the floor between his feet.

"Where's Gigi?"

"She's stayin' another night with her fiancé." He breathed a little fast, as if he'd been running.

"How?" Words wouldn't form.

"Gigi's friend in the travel agency. Cancelled her flight while booking mine at the same time, and…" He lifted one hand and gestured down his body. "Here I am."

"Why?"

"I'm not leaving you on Valentine's Day." His dark gaze locked onto hers. "Not leaving you ever, if I can make you see reason."

"Ever?" What was he proposing? The chance at a life together?

"We have a few hours trapped together on this plane for me to apologize. For me to tell you that I realized…" His jaw worked. "…that I…" His breath hitched. Reaching into the black bag, he pulled out a big, red, heart-shaped balloon. He held it for a moment and handed it to her.

"I love you, Kira. Here's my heart to prove it."

Chills ran through her and shimmied across every inch of her skin. Warmth surrounded her heart and pumped through her veins. She held the balloon tenderly in her hands. "Are you sure?" She hated to be skeptical, but this was too sudden. Especially for a man like Dallas.

"I don't expect you to instantly forgive me, tell me you love me, too, and ask me to marry you before takeoff." His smile was sad. "But please let me talk to you, and…share my feelings with you on the flight."

Dallas Burns? Wanted to share his feelings? "Did you hit your head or something?"

He laughed, low and slow. "I know. Hard to believe this is me talking." He took her hand. "I wanna give us a try." His thumb drew a heart on her palm. "I trust you." His eyes held more emotion than she'd ever seen in him. "I trust you with my heart, Kira."

Tears surged from nowhere and she blinked to keep them from falling. He loved her. Her cowboy loved her and trusted her. Nothing else he could have said would have melted down her resistance the way those words did. "That means a lot to me, Dallas."

She leaned over and kissed him. "I…think I'm falling for you, too."

"Yee-haw!" he called, and pulled her close for a real kiss, a hungry, hot, fast kiss.

"I have something for you, too." Kira whispered it against his lips.

His dark gaze locked with hers. "That kiss was all I needed." He grinned. "For now."

"Mmmm." Would they be able to wait until they reached her apartment to peel off their clothes? She reached for her purse and pulled out the brown envelope. She handed it to him.

"This is what your lawyer gave you." His brow furrowed. Opening the flap, he pulled out an eight by ten color photo. His eyes popped wide. "My grand championship buckle. The one I never found." He swallowed and looked at her. "What is this?"

"Barret's PI spent the better part of last night searching for it. He found where it had been listed and sold online." Here's where her fortune came in handy. "He bought it back and will have it in New York this week. I'll give it to you at the rehearsal dinner…"

Dallas dropped the papers and reached for her. "God, Kira, that's the most incredible thing anyone's ever done for me." Wrapping his arms around her, his face was just inches from hers. "Thank you."

Her chest filled with sweet emotion. "When you told me the story, I knew I had to be the one to find it for you. It's…" She shrugged, trying to contain the love swirling around inside her. "It's my way of helping you heal and get on with your life." He'd dedicated the buckle to his parents. How could he live a full life knowing someone other than him had the buckle?

He cupped her cheek. "You're incredible. I'm lucky."

She laughed. "We both are. Stupid lucky."

"Some of us…" He pointed to his chest. "…are more stupid than others."

"True." She tipped her head. "But smart enough to pull off this caper." She gestured to the space around them.

He leaned in for a kiss but stopped when his phone rang. His gaze fixed on hers. "That's Jayden's ringtone. Okay if I take it? He's going to drive my truck back to Reno."

She nodded and busied herself carefully tucking the splendid heart back into the bag and stowing it under the seat next to her purse. The flight to New York would be intense, the two of them talking through a lot of issues, but for him to even say the things he'd just said was a huge step for him. She'd hear him out. And since there was no chance of his seducing her here on the airplane, she'd be able to make a smart decision. Her eyes rolled at that last thought. As if she'd ever be able to say no to him.

"Jay, you got the keys from Boone?" He listened for a few seconds. "Where are you?" Dallas's lips thinned. Something was wrong. A few seconds went by. "You what?" he snapped. His eyes widened and he looked at Kira. "Did you say married?"

She puffed in a breath and felt the color drain from her face. "Stormie?"

"Jay." Dallas looked at his phone then put it back to his ear. "You there? Jay?" Glancing at the phone again, he shook his head. "Lost him. He's in the mountains."

"Did he really say married?" She held back alarm. Stormie was a grown woman. If they'd done something stupid, her parents would have it fixed.

Dallas's brow furrowed. "I think so. He'll call back after he gets through the pass."

"Wow." She snuggled closer to her cowboy. "And we thought our problems were bad."

He wrapped an arm around her. "All our problems will be fixed by the time we reach NYC."

"Promise?"

He kissed her forehead then drew an X over his chest. "Cross my heart."

The cowboy could be so sweet when he tried. "Thank you for the balloon. It means a lot to me."

He chuckled. "You should have seen me running through the airport in full cowboy gear, blowing up a red balloon. People actually stopped to stare."

Laughter bubbled out of her, and joy at his doing something so conspicuous for her made her weepy again. "I'm sure I'll see a video of it online somewhere."

He sat silently for a moment, considering it. "Could happen." He didn't seem bothered by it.

"If we work things out today…" She already knew they would, but she wanted him to give it his best effort. "You can you stay with me. At my apartment."

"I'm plannin' on it." He tipped his head. "Unless you'd want to keep me hidden from your friends for a while."

"No. I want to show you off…and have you

meet my parents."

His jaw tightened and his lips thinned.

She expected his usual silence.

"Yeah, I'd like to meet them. But I should probably go shopping for something less rustic to wear."

She shook her head. "Oh no. You're perfect just the way you are." She tapped the brim of his hat.

"I want to know everything about your parents. Your family. Tell me everything about your life."

His interest tugged at her heart. "I will. If you'll tell me everything I don't know about you. I want to hear about your business venture with Boone and Gigi, too."

He seemed hesitant for a moment. "While we're in NYC, I wanted to meet with your attorney." He ran his thumb along her chin. "Thank you for talking up the rodeo school to him."

She nipped at his thumb. "I'll go with you. I'd like to hear what he found out about the business."

"Oh, you're comin' with, all right. And we'll be hiring you to be our accountant, once we're at that stage of the business setup."

He wanted her involved in his business? He was serious about bringing her into his life. "I'd love to help."

"But, you may have to move closer to Reno. Like, really close." The hopeful look in his eyes took her breath away.

"Whoa, cowboy. One major shock at a time." She laid her hand on his chest. "You're going to have me seeing double if you keep throwing things like that at me."

"I'll slow down, sweetheart, but not for long. I'm not a patient man." His gaze took in all the features of her face. "Once I commit to something, I'm all-in."

Smiling, she asked, "Promise?"

"Yep."

The flight attendant stopped next to him. "Would you please turn off your phone? We're fifth in line for takeoff."

He pressed the button and slid it into his pocket. "See, Kira? There's another reason you have to take me back. I can't ever hear the phrase 'turn off your phone' without thinking of you."

She sighed and kissed him, her hand on his chest holding tight to the heart she'd never let go of.

####

Jayden and Stormie have their own story, too! It's the third book in the series, Cowboy Jackpot: St. Patrick's Day. Read the book blurb and find out where you can order it on my website, http://randialexander.com/preview/cowboy -jackpot-series-book-3-st-patricks-day/ Here's a sneak peek:

Jayden and Stormie's Story: Cowboy Jackpot: St. Patrick's Day

Chapter One

Jayden Hancock tucked his hand into the rigging on the back of Chicken Foot, the bay gelding he was about to ride bareback. "Who the hell names a horse Chicken Foot?" The object of his derision lurched in the chute, jamming Jayden's leg against the fencing.

The pain shot up his thigh. He had to get loose. He tightened his grip and shouted, "Okay, okay, okay."

Three point eight seconds later, he lay on his back on the hard packed dirt, staring up at the arena ceiling, his breath knocked out of him. He looked up to see the replay of his ride on the big screen above the ring. When it ended, the shot went live to him lying there, his blond, curly hair full of red dirt.

"Fuck." He was careful not to move his lips when he cussed. Someone could easily read his lips on the screen. He scrambled to his feet, picked up his hat and waved to the crowd in gratitude for the few claps and shouts. He heard women's voices woo-hooing as he walked out through the narrow opening between the gates. Gigi, his brother Boone's wife, and Kira, who was long-distance-dating his friend Dallas, were in the stands for the rodeo.

"Great." He pulled off his gloves and stomped back toward the locker room. Now both Kira and Gigi had witnessed his latest failure.

"Tough luck, Jay." His friend Rance smacked him on the back, stirring up a cloud of dirt. "Chicken Foot is a tricky bastard."

"It ain't the horse, it's the rider." He hadn't won an event in months. He rarely hung on for eight seconds. "My head isn't in the right place anymore."

"Bro, don't jinx yourself." Rance's green eyes locked on his. He was big into superstition, and it was working for him. He was getting close to Jayden's brother, Boone, in the bull riding rankings. "Walk it off."

How many times had he heard that in the five months since his rides had turned bad on him? He jerked off his chaps and stuffed them in his gear bag along with his gloves, vest, and spurs. "I'm gonna get a drink. Come with me?"

"I can't, buddy. I'm in the short go." The riders with the best times in the first round faced off in the final round for the win.

He punched Rance on the arm. "Good luck. I'll be cheering for you from the first bar I find."

"Thanks." Rance pulled off his hat and scratched his head, ruffling his black hair. "I'll meet you for a drink after."

Jayden stuffed his gear bag into a locker and secured it. How long had it been since he'd made it to a short go? Too fucking long. His fist connected with the metal door.

"Hey, you've got another chance tomorrow. Concentrate on that." Rance settled his hat low on his head and walked away.

The two-day rodeo at the Old West Casino in Las Vegas drew some of the best riders. If Jayden didn't pull it together and win tomorrow, he'd drop off the bottom of the ranking charts. His pro rodeo career would be over. His credibility to teach bareback riding would be gone. Yeah, his mind wasn't in the right place. Instead of being set on winning, hollow desperation rode shotgun in his head.

Brushing the dirt out of his hair and off his jeans and his unlucky green "lucky shirt," he walked out of the arena into the casino. Poker would take his mind off his troubles. It was the day before Saint Patrick's Day, and he was half Irish. Things should be going in his favor.

He dusted off his brown cowboy hat and set it on his head the way the buckle bunnies liked it, with his curls showing a little around the edges. Maybe finding a sweetie to spend the night with would help him feel luckier.

The poker room was packed, and he put his name on the waiting list for seven card stud. It'd be a while before a spot opened up. He wandered to the snack bar and had a couple tacos and a beer, then found a comfortable seat at a video poker machine.

"Might as well practice." He pulled a twenty out of his wallet and slid it into the machine. It pinged and chirped a welcome. "Dollar poker. Crap." He'd thought it was quarters. What the hell. It was only twenty bucks. He played the maximum, five dollars, and won a few hands.

After he ordered a beer from the cocktail waitress, he looked around the casino. Both his brother Boone and their friend Dallas had met their women here, under very lucky circumstances.

The two of them had pooled their winnings and were in the process of starting a rodeo school where they lived in Reno. Jayden was supposed to be part of the school, but he had no money to fund his piece of the partnership, and was quickly losing his credibility as an expert. No lucky circumstances for him.

The woman he'd met at the casino on Valentine's Day had turned out to be pretty darn unlucky for him personally—if he remembered correctly. It had been a wild night, what he recalled of it. Had they really gotten...? He pushed the scary memory back again, deep behind the beer fog he'd drunken himself into that night. Right now, he just didn't have the willpower to deal with the bad decision he'd made.

His beer came and he focused on his machine, pressing the maximum button as he took a sip from the red plastic cup. Three aces with a five and a seven. Now this was getting interesting.

"Jayden!" A female voice called from a distance.

He glanced around. A buckle bunny? He spotted Stormie Thompson. "Oh man." It was her, his unlucky charm from February.

####

Did you enjoy meeting Boone and Gigi in this book? Would you like to read their story? They star in the first book in the series, Cowboy Jackpot: Christmas. Read the book blurb and find out where you can order it on my website, http://randialexander.com/preview/cowboy -jackpot-christmas/ Here's a sneak peek:

Boone and Gigi's story:
Cowboy Jackpot: Christmas

Chapter One

"Buckle bunnies to your left."

Boone Hancock turned his head at Dallas's alert.

Two cuties stood at one of the giant slot machines. They both smiled and waved.

Dallas tipped back his cowboy hat. "I'm puttin' dibs on the redhead."

Boone glanced at her, but his gaze shot back to the angel with the long black hair and pale skin. Her curves, packed into a petite little body, captured his complete focus. Her slinky purple dress and black spike-heeled sandals shouted she was ready to party.

"Look at those legs." Dallas raised his hand in a return greeting.

The redhead wore a green dress that showed off her nice breasts and skimmed her thin body. Boone smiled. "You like the tall, leggy ones, buddy.

I'm likin' her girlfriend. She's a hot little bundle."

"Let's get 'em." Dallas took a step forward.

"Wait." Boone stopped him with a hand on his shoulder. "Remember, one night. Two at the most."

"Yeah, yeah."

"You say that like you mean it, but we promised to keep each other out of the deep shit."

Dallas looked him square in the eyes. "I learned my lesson the hard way. You don't have to babysit me."

Boone had watched Dallas going through hell two months ago with the girl he thought was the one for him. It had affected his buddy's performance in the arena, and his ability to stay sober.

Boone's little brother, Jayden, caught up to them and busted in between them. "What's going on?"

Dallas nodded toward the two girls. "Couple ladies recognized us and want us to come and say howdy." He flicked the brim of Jaden's cowboy hat. "Now get lost. They're both spoken for."

"Mmm, I'm liking that redhead." Jayden grinned at her.

Boone looked back at the women. The shorter one—his—waved them over.

"Called dibs." Dallas hitched up his jeans and headed toward the girls.

Jayden caught up to him. "We'll see, won't we."

Boone quick-stepped and lined up next to his brother. As they got closer, he saw his cutie's eyes watching him. Hazel. Damn. Beautiful eyes, beautiful face, a body that he needed tight against his. It didn't take any effort to slide into charming cowboy mode.

His body warmed, primed and ready to sweet-talk this little honey 'till her toes curled.

****

Gieselle Colberg-Staub leaned against the Birthday Baby slot machine, her knees wobbly and her stomach jittering as she watched Boone Hancock walk toward her. "I can't believe it. They're actually coming over here."

Kira twirled a lock of hair around one finger and made a shy smile at the cowboys. "Of course they're coming over here. How could they resist?"

Gieselle sucked in a calming breath. She'd watched Boone win the bull riding competition this afternoon, and now he—and his big, shiny belt buckle—headed her way. "God, he's cute." Shaggy blonde hair touched his collar at the back of his black cowboy hat. A purple and black print western shirt and the sexiest jeans she'd ever seen on a man.

"That big, dark haired hunk is fucking gorgeous." Kira sipped her vodka tonic.

"That's Dallas Burns. He came in third in bareback riding today." She glanced at her friend. "Weren't you watching?"

Kira sniffed. "You saw that sexy cowboy sitting right behind us. He was worth watching."

Gieselle had picked up a love of rodeo from her college roommate, but this was the first live event she'd attended. Now the sexy stars she'd drooled over headed straight toward her. She held back a nervous giggle. "Dallas is definitely your type with those dark eyes."

"Oh yes, my heart is thumping." Kira stirred the ice in her drink with the straw. "So, we agree? Dallas for me and Boone for you?"

Gieselle licked her lips. She would let herself go a little crazy this holiday break, because what happens in Vegas, hopefully stays in Vegas. "Agreed." She squinted. "What about the third one?"

Kira laughed. "Oh, now you're getting kinky?"

Gieselle sent her a look. "That's your specialty, girl."

The cowboys reached them, sauntering up with wicked grins on their faces, like they expected Kira and her to peel down naked and let them have a quickie right here on the casino floor.

Gieselle liked the cockiness.

#####

Connect With Me

Thank you for reading the second Cowboy Jackpot story. I loved creating two such different characters in Kira and Dallas. Opposites do attract!. I'd love to hear from you. I've listed all the places I hang out, and I hope you'll connect with me at one or more of them.

All my best,

Randi

"Rode Hard and Put Up Satisfied"

http://RandiAlexander.com

https://www.facebook.com/RandiAlexanderAuthor

http://twitter.com/Randi_Alexander

http://www.goodreads.com/author/show/4885056.Randi_Alexander

http://wildandwickedcowboys.wordpress.com/

http://69shadesofsmut.wordpress.com/

About the Author

Randi Alexander is published with The Wild Rose Press Cowboy Kink line and with Cleis Press. When she's not dreaming of, or writing about, kinky cowboys, she's biking trails along remote rivers, snorkeling the Gulf of Mexico, or practicing her drumming in hopes of someday forming a tropical-rock band.

Other Books by Randi Alexander

Available Now:

Chase and Seduction - Country music superstar/actor Chase Tanner has yet to be denied anything—and he's never wanted anything or anyone more than gorgeous screenplay writer Reno Linden. So when the film they are working on is finally finished, Chase decides to turn up the volume on seducing Reno.

Reno Linden lived a quiet, rural life until she was thrust into the Hollywood scene when her book was adapted to film. Chase Tanner is larger than life, sinfully sexy and hell-bent on getting her into bed. Skittish after a failed wedding engagement, Reno risks the plunge into Chase's arms, and is surprised that her good girl self can keep up with bad boy Chase.

Though Chase returns to his cowboy roots often, and Reno cherishes the time spent with him on his ranch, the two find their careers pulling them in different directions. Will their attraction survive the glitz and stress of fame?

Her Cowboy Stud - Trace McGonagall's quiet life on his Houston stud ranch is shaken up when gorgeous Macy Veralta arrives to claim an inheritance left to her in his uncle's will. Trace sees her as just another gold digger, but he also can't resist her curvy body. When she hints at being the perfect submissive to his Dom, he has to have her.

Macy wouldn't have been three months late to

claim her inheritance if she'd known Trace was sin in jeans. The cowboy's dominant bearing and the smoldering glint in his eyes send shivers to her toes and stirs images of being bound in his bed and disciplined at his hand. But could Trace's perfect seduction be part of his plan to reclaim her inheritance?

Turn Up the Heat - During the filming of the reality show America's Newest Chef, finalist Mackenzie Jarvis falls desperately in lust with actress Gina Volto. Mackenzie's never been with a woman, and her strict Wyoming upbringing has her questioning whether she can loosen up enough to live out her fantasy.

When Gina shows Mackenzie how sensual their nights could be, Mackenzie ignores her doubts for one wild weekend. Monday morning, she returns home to her ranch, her horses, and her busy career as the owner and chef of a restaurant. But a week later Gina shows up at Mackenzie's home. She's come to Wyoming-for Mackenzie.

Gina teaches Mackenzie the sweet pleasures of loving a woman, the naughty sting of a whip, and the seductive submission of bondage. But Gina admits she wants more than just a few days. Can conservative, family-valued Mackenzie ignore the plans she's made for her life, and find her future in the tender arms of a woman?

Cowboy Bad Boys - Randi Alexander has created ten male/ female (M/F) erotic romances starring sexy cowboys and the ladies in their lives. Each story combines the heart-pounding heat you expect from

Randi, as well as the touching romance she does so well. Randi's stories take you from an early summer High Country Ride in the Rockies, to a dangerous buck off a rodeo bull with a Hard Headed Cowboy.

Body Heat – When a rancher and his gorgeous passenger are buried in his truck under an avalanche, they discover a sensual way to keep warm.

Breakfast in Bed – A ranch foreman devises a plan to keep his woman from bolting out of his bed every time they're through making love.

Hard Headed Cowboy – When a rodeo bull rider needs a lift, his sexy equipment sponsor makes him a proposition.

High Country Ride – Fulfilling her father's last wishes, a city girl hires a hot cowboy to guide her into the Rockies.

Kill Me or Kiss Me – With her life in danger, an exotic dancer has to trust a sexy cattle rustler to keep her alive.

No Way Out – The town sheriff and the beautiful bank president he's been lusting after are cornered by a killer.

Private Lessons – When her girlfriends buy her a mechanical bull lesson with a real bull rider, a college girl gets a sensual ride from her high school crush.

Stubborn Redhead – The rancher's woman left him because of rumors of his cheating, but what will it take to make her believe his innocence?

Takin' a Chance – A barrel racer has one last opportunity to seduce the sexy rodeo bullfighter she's fallen for.

Where We Left Off – In desperate need of help, a country veterinarian contacts the man she'd loved but booted out of her life years ago.

Banging the Cowboy (short story in the Cowboy Lust anthology) - Every Saturday for a year, Annie Paris has lusted after Rafe McCord from behind her drumset on stage at the honky tonk. The Big Cowboy, they call him, and rumors say he likes it rough in the bedroom. The thought of banging him makes Annie's pussy tingle and cream.

But Rafe is a one-night-stand kind of guy, and Annie couldn't handle seeing him every Saturday, knowing she'd already had her one night with him. That there'd be no more.

Tonight, something's different. Rafe doesn't leave with a woman. And he's been staring at Annie since he came in the door. At closing time, he sets his longneck on the bar, and swaggers toward her, his gaze locked on hers, his smile pure sexual invitation. Annie's slit contracts and her nipples harden. Oh, God, if he asks her to his house for a rough ride on his big, hard cock, where would she find the strength to say "no"?

Coming Soon:

Double Her Fantasy - At a comic book convention, artist Megan Shore is thrilled to meet action movie hunk Garret McGatlin. Usually reclusive, Megan flirts with the leading man of her sexual fantasies. He invites her to his suite for a drink, but when she arrives, his rancher brother Trey opens the door and unleashes Megan's cowboy fantasy. Both men pour on the charm, and she can't decide which of them she desires more.

The McGatlin brothers have shared women, but none of them were like Megan, irresistible and perfect for both of them. Working together, they execute a potent seduction. During a hot, amazing week, the three-way relationship becomes emotionally charged. When they're thrown into the media spotlight, Megan fears the exposure will trigger a past threat. Garrett and Trey need to prove they can keep Megan safe as well as happy and satisfied in their arms.

19530816R00072

Made in the USA
Charleston, SC
29 May 2013